The Rover Boys In Business Or, The Search For The Missing Bonds

by

Arthur M. Winfield

Double 9
BOOKS

The Rover Boys In Business
Or, The Search For The Missing Bonds
by Arthur M. Winfield

ISBN: 978-93-57272-98-8

Published by

DOUBLE 9 BOOKS

2/13-B, Ansari Road
Daryaganj, New Delhi – 110002
info@double9books.com
www.double9books.com
Tel. 011-40042856

ABOUT THE AUTHOR

Arthur M. Winfield (Edward Stratemeyer) was born on October 4, 1862, to Henry Julius Stratemeyer a tobacconist, and Anna Siegel. He was an American publisher, writer of Children's fiction, and founder of the Stratemeyer Syndicate. He was probably the most creative author in the world, producing over 1,300 books and selling over 500 million copies. He also created many famous fictional book series for juveniles, including The Rover boys, The Bobbsey Twins, Tom Swift, The Hardy boys, and Nancy Drew. As a teenager, Stratemeyer worked at his own printing press in the basement of his father's tobacco shop, distributing flyers and brochures to his relatives. These included stories titled The Newsboys Adventure and The Tale of a Lumberman. After graduating from high school, he worked in his father's shop. He is not even 26 in 1888 while Stratemeyer sold his first story Victor Horton's Idea, to the famous children magazine The Golden Days.

CONTENTS

INTRODUCTION

My Dear Boys: This book is a complete story in itself, but forms the nineteenth volume in a line issued under the general title of "The Rover Boys Series for Young Americans."

As I have mentioned in several other volumes, this series was started a number of years ago with the publication of "The Rover Boys at School," "On the Ocean," and "In the Jungle." I am happy to say the books were so well liked that they were followed, year after year, by the publication of "The Rover Boys Out West," "On the Great Lakes," "In Camp," "On Land and Sea," "On the River," "On the Plains," "In Southern Waters," "On the Farm," "On Treasure Isle," "At College," "Down East," "In the Air," "In New York," and finally "In Alaska," where we last met the lads.

During all these adventures the Rover boys have been growing older. Dick is now married and conducting his father's business in New York City and elsewhere. 'The fun-loving Tom and his sturdy younger brother, Sam, are at Brill College. The particulars are given of a great baseball game; and then Tom and Sam return home, to be startled by a most unusual message from Dick, calling them to New York immediately. Some bonds of great value have mysteriously disappeared, and unless these are recovered the Rover fortune may be seriously impaired. What the boys did under these circumstances, I will leave the pages which follow to disclose.

Once more thanking my host of young readers for the interest they have taken in my books, I remain,

Affectionately and sincerely yours,

Arthur M. Winfield.

CHAPTER I.
AT THE RIVER

"Sam!"

No answer.

"I say, Sam, can't you listen for just a moment?"

"Oh, Tom, please don't bother me now!" and Sam Rover, with a look of worry on his face, glanced up for a moment from his writing-table. "I've got to finish this theme before to-morrow morning."

"Oh, I know! But listen!" And Tom Rover's face showed his earnestness. "Last night it was full moonlight, and to-night it is going to be equally clear. Why can't we get out the auto and pay a visit to Hope? You know we promised the girls that we would be up some afternoon or evening this week."

"Sounds good, Tom, but even if we went after, supper, could we get there in time? You know all visitors have to leave before nine o'clock."

"We can get there if we start as soon as we finish eating. Can't you finish the theme after we get back? Maybe I can help you."

"Help me? On this theme!" Sam grinned broadly. "Tom, you don't know what you are talking about. Do you know what this theme is on?"

"No, but I can help you if I have to."

"This is on 'The Theory Concerning the Evolution of— —'"

"That's enough, Sam; don't give me any of it now. Time enough for that when we have to get at it. There goes the supper bell. Now, downstairs with you! and let us get through as soon as possible and be on our way."

"All right, just as you say!" and gathering up a number of sheets of paper, Sam thrust them in the drawer of the writing-table.

"By the way, it's queer we didn't get any letter to-day from Dick," the youngest Rover observed.

At the mention of their brother's name, Tom's face clouded a little.

"It is queer, Sam, and I must say I don't like it. I think this is a case where no news is bad news. I think if everything was going along all right in New York, Dick would surely let us know. I am afraid he is having a good deal of trouble in straightening out Dad's business."

"Just the way I look at it," responded Sam, as the brothers prepared to leave the room.

"One thing is sure, Pelter, Japson & Company certainly did all they could to mix matters up, and I doubt very much if they gave Dad all that was coming to him."

"I believe I made a mistake in coming back to college," pursued Tom, as the two boys walked out into the corridor, where they met several other students on the way to the dining hall. "I think I ought to have given up college and gone to New York City to help Dick straighten out that business tangle. Now that Dad is sick again, the whole responsibility rests on Dick's shoulders, and he ought not to be made to bear it alone."

"Well, if you feel that way, Tom, why don't you break away and go? I think, perhaps, it would be not only a good thing for Dick, but it would, also, be a good thing for you," and, for the moment, Sam looked very seriously at his brother.

Tom reddened a bit, and then put his forefinger to his forehead. "You mean it would help me here?" And then, as Sam nodded, he added: "Oh, don't you worry. I am all right now, my head doesn't bother me a bit. But I do wish I could get just one good chance at Pelter for the crack that rascal gave me on the head with the footstool."

"It certainly was a shame to let him off, Tom, but you know how father felt about it. He was too sick to be worried by a trial at law and all that."

"Yes, I know, but just the same, some day I am going to square accounts with Mr. Jesse Pelter," and Tom shook his head determinedly.

Passing down the broad stairway of Brill College, the two Rover boys made their way to the dining hall. Here the majority of the students were rapidly assembling for the evening meal, and the lads found themselves among a host of friends.

"Hello, Songbird! How are you this evening?" cried Tom, as he addressed a tall, scholarly-looking individual who wore his hair rather long. "Have you been writing any poetry to-day?"

"Well,—er—not exactly, Tom," muttered John Powell, otherwise known as Songbird because of his numerous efforts to compose what he called poetry. "But I have been thinking up a few rhymes."

"When are you going to get out that book of poetry?"

"What book is that, Tom?"

"Why, as if you didn't know! Didn't you tell me that you were going to get up a volume of 'Original International Poems for the Grave and Gay;' five hundred pages, fully illustrated; and bound in full leather, with title in gold, and..."

"Tom, Tom, now please stop your fooling!" pleaded Songbird, his face flushing. "Just because I write a poem now and then doesn't say that I am going to publish a book."

"No, but I'm sure you will some day, and you'll make a fortune out of it—or fifteen dollars, anyway."

"The same old Tom!" cried a merry voice, and another student clapped the fun-loving Rover on the shoulder. "I do believe you would rather joke than eat!"

"Not on your life, Spud! and I'll prove it to you right now!" and linking his arm through that of Will Jackson, otherwise "Spud," Tom led the way to one of the tables, with Sam and several of the other students following.

"What is on the docket for to-night?" asked Songbird, as he fell to eating.

"Tom and I are going to take a little run in the auto to Hope," answered Sam.

"Oh, I see!" Songbird Powell shut one eye knowingly. "Going up there to see the teachers, I suppose!"

"Sure, that is what they always do!" came from Spud, with a wink.

"Sour grapes, Spud!" laughed Sam. "You would go there yourself if you had half a chance."

"Yes, and Songbird would want to go along, too, if we were bound for the Sanderson cottage," put in Tom. "You see, in Songbird's eyes, Minnie Sanderson is just the nicest girl— —"

"Now stop it, Tom, can't you!" pleaded poor Songbird, growing decidedly red in the face. "Miss Sanderson is only a friend of mine, and you know it."

Just at that moment the students at the table were interrupted by the approach of a tall, dudish-looking individual, who wore a reddish-brown suit, cut in the most up-to-date fashion, and who sported patent-leather shoes, and a white carnation in his buttonhole. The newcomer took a vacant chair, sitting down with a flourish.

"I've had a most delightful ramble, don't you know," he lisped, looking around at the others. "I have been through the sylvan woods and by the babbling brook, and have——"

"Great Caesar's tombstone!" exclaimed Tom, looking at the newcomer critically. "Why, my dearly beloved William Philander, you don't mean to say that you have been delving through the shadowy nooks, and playing with the babbling brook, in that outfit?"

"Oh, dear, no, Tom!" responded William Philander Tubbs. "I had another suit on, the one with the green stripe, don't you know,—the one I had made last September—or maybe it was in October, I can't really remember. But you must know the suit, don't you?"

"Sure! I remember the suit. The green-striped one with the faded-out blue dots and the red diamond check in the corner. Isn't that the same suit you took down to the pawnbroker's last Wednesday night at fifteen minutes past seven and asked him to loan you two dollars and a half on it, and the pawnbroker wanted to know if the suit was your own?"

"My dear Tom!" and William Philander looked aghast. "You know well enough I never took that suit to a pawnbroker."

"Well, maybe it was some other suit. Possibly the black one with the blue stripes, or maybe it was the blue one with the black stripes. Really, my dearest Philander, it is immaterial to me what suit it was." And Tom looked coldly indifferent as he buttered another slice of bread.

"But I tell you, I never went to any pawn-broker!" pleaded the dudish student. "I would not be seen in any such horrid place!"

"Oh, pawnbrokers are not so bad," came from Spud Jackson, as he helped himself to more potatoes. "I knew of one fellow down in New Haven who used to loan thousands of dollars to the students at Yale.

He was considered a public benefactor. When he died they closed up the college for three days and gave him a funeral over two miles long. And after that, the students raised a fund of sixteen thousand dollars with which to erect a monument to his memory. Now, that is absolutely true, and if you don't believe it you can come to my room and I will show you some dried rose leaves which came from one of the wreathes used at the obsequies." And a general laugh went up over this extravagant statement.

"The same old Spud!" cried Sam, as he gave the story-teller of the college a nudge in the ribs. "Spud, you are about as bad as Tom."

"Chust vat I tinks," came from Max Spangler, a German-American student who was still struggling with the difficulties of the language. "Only I tinks bod of dem vas worser dan de udder." And at this rather mixed statement another laugh went up.

"I wish you fellows would stop your nonsense and talk baseball," came from Bob Grimes, another student. "Do you realize that if we expect to do anything this spring, we have got to get busy?"

"Well, Bob," returned Sam, "I don't see how that is going to interest me particularly. I don't expect to be on any nine this year."

"I know, Sam, but Tom, here, has promised to play if he can possibly get the time."

"And so I will play," said Tom. "That is, provided I remain at Brill."

"What, do you mean to say you are going to leave!" cried several students.

"We can't do without you, Tom," added Songbird.

"Of course we can't," came from Bob Grimes. "We need Tom the worst way this year."

"Well, I'll talk that over with you fellows some other time. To-night we are in a hurry." And thus speaking, Tom tapped his brother on the shoulder, and both left the dining-room.

As my old readers know, the Rover boys possessed a very fine automobile. This was kept in one of the new garages on the place, which was presided over by Abner Filbury, the son of the old man who had worked for years around the dormitories.

"Is she all ready, Ab?" questioned Tom, as the young man came forward to greet them.

"Yes, sir, I filled her up with gas and oil, and she's in apple-pie order."

"Why, Tom!" broke in Sam, in surprise. "You must have given this order before supper."

"I did," and Tom grinned at his younger brother. "I took it for granted that you would make the trip." And thus speaking, Tom leaped into the driver's seat of the new touring car. Then Sam took his place beside his brother, and in a moment more the car was gliding out of the garage, and down the curving, gravel path leading to the highway running from Ashton past Brill College to Hope Seminary.

As Tom had predicted, it was a clear night, with the full moon just showing over the distant hills. Swinging into the highway, Tom increased the speed and was soon running at twenty-five to thirty miles an hour.

"Don't run too fast," cautioned Sam. "Remember this road has several dangerous curves in it, and remember, too, a good many of the countrymen around here don't carry lights when they drive."

"Oh, I'll be careful," returned Tom, lightly. "But about the lights, I think some of the countrymen ought to be fined for driving in the darkness as they do. I think— —"

"Hark! what sort of a noise is that?" interrupted the younger Rover.

Both boys strained their ears. A shrill honk of a horn had been followed by a heavy rumble, and now, around a curve of the road, shot the beams from a single headlight perched on a heavy auto-truck. This huge truck was coming along at great speed, and it passed the Rovers with a loud roar, and a scattering of dust and small stones in all directions.

"Great Scott!" gasped Sam, after he had recovered from his amazement. "Did you ever see such an auto-truck as that, and running at such speed?"

"Certainly some truck," was Tom's comment. "That must have weighed four or five tons. I wonder if it came over the Paxton River bridge?"

"If it did, it must have given the bridge an awful shaking up. That bridge isn't any too strong. It shakes fearfully every time we go over it. Better run slow, Tom, when we get there."

"I will." And then Tom put on speed once more and the automobile forged ahead as before.

A short run up-hill brought them to the point where the road ran down to the Paxton River. In the bright moonlight the boys could see the stream flowing like a sheet of silver down between the bushes and trees. A minute more, and they came in sight of the bridge.

"Stop!" said Sam. "I may be mistaken, but that bridge looks shifted to me."

"So it does," returned Tom, and brought the automobile to a standstill. Both boys leaped out and walked forward.

To inspect the bridge in the bright moonlight was easy, and in less than a minute the boys made a startling discovery, which was to the effect that the opposite end of the structure had been thrown from its supports and was in danger of falling at any instant.

"This is mighty bad," was Sam's comment. "Why, Tom, this is positively dangerous. If anybody should come along here——"

"Hark!" Tom put up his hand, and both boys listened. From the top of the hill they had left but a moment before, came the sounds of an approaching automobile. An instant later the rays of the headlights shot into view, almost blinding them.

"We must stop them!" came from both boys simultaneously. But scarcely had the words left their lips, when they saw that such a course might be impossible. The strange automobile was coming down the hill at a furious rate. Now, as the driver saw the Rovers' machine, he sounded his horn shrilly.

"He'll have a smash-up as sure as fate!" yelled Sam, and put up his hand in warning. Tom did likewise, and also yelled at the top of his lungs.

But it was too late. The occupant of the strange automobile—for the machine carried but a single person—tried to come to a stop. The brakes groaned and squeaked, and the car swept slightly to one side, thus avoiding the Rovers' machine. Then, with power thrown off and the hand-brake set, it rolled out on the bridge. There was a snap, followed by a tremendous crash, and the next instant machine and driver disappeared with a splash into the swiftly-flowing river.

CHAPTER II.
TO THE RESCUE

The accident at the bridge had occurred so suddenly that, for the instant, neither Rover boy knew what to do. They saw that the farther end of the bridge had given way completely. Just where the end rested in the water they beheld several small objects floating about, one of them evidently a cap, and another a small wooden box. But the automobile with its driver was nowhere to be seen.

"My gracious! That fellow will surely be drowned!" gasped Sam, on recovering from the shock. "Tom, do you see him anywhere?"

"No, I don't." Tom took a few steps forward and gazed down into the swiftly-flowing stream. "Perhaps he is pinned under the auto, Sam!"

"Wait, I'll get the searchlight," cried the younger Rover, and ran back to their automobile. The boys made a point of carrying an electric pocket searchlight to be used in case they had to make repairs in the dark. Securing this, and turning on the light, Sam ran forward to the river bank, with Tom beside him.

To those who have read the previous volumes in this "Rover Boys Series" the lads just mentioned will need no special introduction. For the benefit of others, however, let me state that the Rover boys were three in number; Dick being the oldest, fun-loving Tom coming next, and sturdy Sam being the youngest. When at home, which was only for a short time each year, the boys lived with their father, Anderson Rover, and their Uncle Randolph and Aunt Martha on a farm called Valley Brook, in New York State.

While their father was in Africa, the boys had been sent to Putnam Hall Military Academy, as related in the first volume of this series, entitled "The Rover Boys at School." There they had made quite a few friends, and, also, some enemies.*

*For particulars regarding how Putnam Hall Military Academy was organized, and what fine times the cadets there enjoyed even before the Rovers appeared on the scene, read "The Putnam Hall Series," six volumes, starting with "The Putnam Hall Cadets." — Publishers

The first term at school was followed by an exciting trip on the ocean, and then another trip into the jungles of Africa, where the boys went looking for their parent. Then came a journey to the West, and some grand times on the Great Lakes and in the Mountains. After that, the Rover boys came back to the Hall to go into camp with their fellow-cadets. Then they took a long journey over land and sea, being cast away on a lonely island in the Pacific.

On returning home, the boys had imagined they were to settle down to a quiet life, but such was not to be. On a houseboat the lads, with some friends, sailed down the Ohio and the Mississippi rivers, and then found themselves on the Plains, where they solved the mystery of Red Rock ranch. Then they set sail on Southern Waters, and in the Gulf of Mexico discovered a deserted yacht.

"Now for a good rest," Sam had said, and the three lads had returned to the home farm, where, quite unexpectedly, more adventures befell them. Then they returned to Putnam Hall; and all graduated with considerable honor.

It had been decided by Mr. Rover that the boys should next go to college, and he selected an institution of learning located in the Middle West, not far from the town of Ashton. Brill College was a fine place, and the Rovers knew they would like it as soon as they saw it. With them went their old-time school chum, Songbird Powell, already mentioned. At the same time, William Philander Tubbs came to the college from Putnam Hall. He was a dudish fellow, who thought far more of dress than of gaining an education, and he was often made the butt of some practical joke.

It did not take the Rover boys long to make a number of friends at Brill. These included Stanley Browne, a tall, gentlemanly youth; Bob Grimes, who was greatly interested in baseball and other sports; Max Spangler, a German-American youth, who was everybody's friend; and Will Jackson, always called "Spud" because of his unusual fondness for potatoes. Spud was a great story-teller, and some of his yarns were marvelous in the extreme.

During their first term at Putnam Hall, the Rover boys had become well acquainted with Dora Stanhope, who lived near the school with her widowed mother, and, also, Nellie and Grace Laning, Dora's two cousins, who resided but a short distance further away. It had not been long before Dick and Dora showed a great liking for each other, and, at the same time, Tom often "paired off" with Nellie, and Sam as often sought the company of Grace. Then came the time when the boys did a great service for Mrs. Stanhope, saving her from the wicked plotting of Josiah Crabtree, a teacher at Putnam Hall. Crabtree was exposed, and lost no time in leaving the school, threatening at the same time that, sooner or later, he would "square accounts with the Rovers."

But a few miles away from Brill College was located Hope Seminary, an institution for girls. When the Rover boys went to Brill, Dora, Nellie and Grace entered Hope, so the young folks met almost as often as before. A term at Brill was followed by an unexpected trip Down East, where the Rover boys again brought the rascally Crabtree to terms. Then the lads became the possessors of a biplane, and took several thrilling trips through the air. About this time, Mr. Anderson Rover, who was not in the best of health, was having much trouble with some brokers, who were trying to swindle him out of valuable property. He went to New York City, and disappeared, and his three sons went at once on the hunt for him. The brokers were Pelter, Japson & Company, and it was not long before Dick and his brothers discovered that Pelter and Japson were in league with Josiah Crabtree. In the end the boys found out what had become of their parent, and they managed to bring the brokers to terms. But, during a struggle, poor Tom was hit on the head by a wooden footstool thrown by Pelter, and knocked unconscious. Josiah Crabtree tried to escape from a garret window by means of a rope made of a blanket. This broke, and he sustained a heavy fall, breaking a leg in two places. He was taken to a hospital, and the doctors there said he would be a cripple for life.

"There is no use in talking, Dad," Dick had said to his father, "you are not in a fit physical condition to take hold of these business matters. You had better leave them entirely to me." And to this Mr. Rover had agreed. Then, as Dick was to leave college and spend most of his time in New York, it had been decided that he and Dora should get married. There had followed one of the grandest weddings the village of Cedarville had ever seen.

The blow on Tom's head proved more serious than was at first anticipated. Through it the poor lad suddenly lost his mind, and while in that state he wandered away from Brill College, and went on a long journey, as related in detail in the volume preceding this, entitled "The Rover Boys in Alaska."

As their father was too ill to take part in any search for the missing one, Dick and Sam took up the hunt, and after many thrilling adventures on the ice and in the snow, managed to locate their brother and bring him back home.

"And now, Tom, you must take a good long rest," his kindly Aunt Martha had said, and she had insisted upon it that he be put under the care of a specialist. Tom had rested for several months, and then, declaring that he felt as good as ever, had returned to Brill. Sam was already in the grind, and soon Tom was doing his best to make up for the time he had lost on his strange trip.

Of course, Nellie Laning had been very much worried over Tom's condition, and his disappearance had caused her intense dismay. Since he had returned to Brill, she had asked that he either call on her or write to her at least once a week. Tom preferred a visit to letter-writing, and as Sam was usually ready to go to Hope to see Grace whenever the opportunity afforded, the brothers usually took the trip together, as in the present instance.

Searchlight in hand, the Rover boys peered out over the surface of the swiftly-flowing river, which at this point was about seventy-five feet wide. The bridge was built in three sections, and it was the middle span which had collapsed at the farther end, so that the automobile had plunged into water which was at least eight feet deep.

"Do you see anything of him?" asked Sam, eagerly, as the rays from the light flashed in one direction and then in another.

"If he managed to get out of the auto, perhaps he floated down with the current," responded his brother. "Anyhow, he doesn't seem to be around here."

"Maybe he was caught under the wheel. If so, we had better get him out without delay."

"Look! Look!" And now Tom pointed down the river. There in the moonlight, both boys saw a form coming to the surface. The fellow was beating the water wildly with his hands, and now he set up a frantic cry for aid. Turning the searchlight in that direction, the Rover boys left the vicinity of the broken bridge, and made their way down to something of a footpath that ran along the water's edge. Tom was in the lead. Here and there the bushes hung over the stream, and both lads had to scramble along as best they could.

"Help! Help!" The cry came faintly, and then the two boys saw the fellow in the water throw up both arms and sink from view.

"He has gone under!" gasped Sam. "Hurry up, Tom, or we'll be too late!"

Scrambling wildly through the last of the bushes and onto some flat rocks that, in this vicinity, ran out into the river, the Rover boys soon gained a point which was less than four yards from where the unfortunate youth had disappeared. Leading the way, Tom leaped from one flat stone in the stream to another. Sam followed closely, holding the searchlight on the spot where both hoped the fellow in the water might reappear.

"Here he is!" cried Tom. And, as he spoke, Sam saw a dark object turn over in the stream close to the rock on which his brother had leaped. The next instant Tom was down on his knees and feeling through the water.

"Hold my hand, Sam," said the older Rover. And as Sam took his left hand, Tom clutched with his right the coat of the party in the river. Then came a hard pull; and a moment later Tom had the dripping form on the rock.

"Is he—he—dead?" questioned Sam, hoarsely.

"I don't think so, but he certainly has had a close call. We must get him ashore and work over him as soon as possible. You light the way; I think I can carry him alone."

The fellow who had been hauled out of the river was a slightly-built youth, not over twenty years of age. As Tom was both big and muscular, it was an easy matter for him to throw the stranger over his shoulder. Sam led the way to the shore, keeping the light down on the rocks so that his brother might be sure of his footing.

Once safe, the boys placed the stranger on the grass and started to work over him. He was unconscious, and had evidently swallowed considerable water. Fortunately, the lads had taken lessons in how to resuscitate a person who had been close to drowning, so they knew exactly what to do.

"It's a mighty lucky thing that we were here to aid him," remarked Sam, as he and Tom proceeded with their efforts. "Another minute, and it would have been all up with this poor fellow."

"Well, he isn't out of the woods yet, Sam, but I think he is coming around." And even as Tom spoke the stranger gave a gasp and a groan, and tried to sit up.

"It's all right, my friend," cried Sam, reassuringly. "We've got you, you are safe."

"Oh, oh!" moaned the young man who had been so close to drowning. And then as he sat up and stared at the brothers, he added: "Did—did you sa—save me?"

"Well, we hauled you out of the river," replied Tom, simply.

"You did!" The young man shivered as he glanced at the swiftly-flowing stream. "The bridge—it was broken, but I didn't notice it in time."

"We tried to warn you," said Sam, "but you were coming too fast."

"I know it, but I—I——" And then the young man, having tried to get to his feet, suddenly collapsed and became unconscious again.

"Phew!" came from Sam in surprise. "He must be worse off than we thought."

"Perhaps he got struck when he went down," suggested Tom. "See here, there is blood on his hand; it is running down his sleeve!"

"Maybe his arm is broken, Tom. I guess the best thing we can do is to get him to some doctor."

"Why not take him right down to Ashton to Doctor Havens?"

"Good idea; we'll do it."

Tom again took up the unconscious young man, and, with Sam leading the way, both hurried to their automobile. The stranger was deposited on the seat of the tonneau, and then Tom lost no time in turning the machine around and heading for town.

"I wonder who he can be?" remarked Sam, as they sped along.

"I'm sure I don't know," was Tom's reply. Neither of the boys dreamed of the surprise in store for them.

CHAPTER III.
SOMETHING OF A SURPRISE

It did not take the Rover boys long to reach Ashton; and once in town, they lost no time in running their auto to where Doctor Havens resided. They found the house well lit up, and the old doctor in his study, poring over some medical works.

"Saved a fellow from drowning, eh?" he queried, after the lads had explained matters. "Got him out in your auto? All right, bring him right in if you want to—or wait, I'll go out and take a look at him. Maybe I know who he is and where he belongs." And thus speaking, the doctor went outside.

Sam still had the searchlight in hand, and as the physician approached the automobile, the lad flashed the rays on the face of the stranger, who was still unconscious.

"Why, I've seen that young chap before!" exclaimed Doctor Havens. "He is stopping at the hotel. I saw him there only this afternoon."

"Then perhaps we had better take him over there," suggested Tom.

"By all means, and I'll go with you."

Running into the house, the doctor procured his hand case, and then joined the boys in the automobile. A run of a few minutes brought the party to the hotel, and Sam and Tom lifted the young man out and carried him inside.

The arrival of the party created some consternation, but as only the proprietor of the hotel and a bellboy were present, the matter was kept rather quiet. The young man had a room on the second floor, and to this he was speedily taken, and placed in the care of the doctor.

"No bones broken so far as I can ascertain," said Doctor Havens, after a long examination. "He has cut his forehead, and he also has a bruise behind his left ear, but I think he is suffering more from shock than anything else."

"Did you say you knew him?" questioned Tom.

"Oh, no, only that I had seen him around this hotel."

"What is his name?" asked Sam, of the hotel proprietor, who had followed them to the room.

"His name is Pelter."

"Pelter!" The cry came from Tom and Sam simultaneously, and the brothers looked at each other questioningly.

"Yes, Pelter. Do you know him?"

"What is his first name?" demanded Tom.

"Why, let me see," The hotel man mused for a moment. "I have it! Barton Pelter."

"I never heard that name before," said Tom. "We know a man in——" And then, as Sam looked at him in a peculiar way, he added, "Oh, well, never mind. We don't know this fellow, anyway. I hope he gets over this trouble."

By this time the sufferer had again recovered consciousness, but he was evidently very weak, and the doctor motioned for the Rover boys and the hotel man to leave the room.

"All right, but let us know in the morning by telephone how he is, Doctor," returned Tom; and then the Rover boys and the hotel man went below.

"Can you tell us anything about this Barton Pelter?" questioned Sam, of the proprietor.

"I know very little about him, excepting that he is registered as from Brooklyn, and that he came here three days ago. What his business is in Ashton, I haven't the least idea."

"Is he well off—that is, does he appear to have much money?" asked Tom.

"Oh, he hasn't shown any great amount of cash around here," laughed the hotel man. "My idea is that he is some sort of a commercial traveler, although he hasn't anything with him but his suitcase."

This was all the hotel man could tell them, and a few minutes later the Rover boys were in their automobile once more and headed back for the scene of the accident.

"We ought to have put up some danger signal, Tom," remarked Sam, while on the way.

"I know it, but we hadn't any time to waste while we had that poor chap on our hands. By the way, do you think he can be any relative of Jesse Pelter, the rascal who knocked me out with the footstool, and who tried his best to rob dad?"

"I'm sure I don't know. One thing is certain: The name of Pelter is not common. Still, there may be other Pelters besides those related to that scoundrel of a broker."

Arriving at the vicinity of the broken bridge, the boys found a farmer with a wagon there. The countryman was placing some brushwood across the road.

"The blame bridge is busted down," said the farmer, "and I thought I ought to put up some kind of a thing to warn folks of it."

"That is what we came for," answered Sam; and then he and his brother related some of the particulars of what had occurred.

"Gee, shoo! You don't mean to tell me that one of them automobiles is down in the river!" gasped the countryman. "I don't see nothin' of it."

"It most be down on the bottom, close to where that end of the bridge settled," answered Sam "I suppose there will be a job here for somebody to haul it out."

"If they want a man for that, I'm the feller to do it," returned the countryman. "Maybe I had better go down to the hotel and see about it."

"Better wait till morning," suggested Tom. "The young man who owns the machine can't see anyone now."

"All right, just as you say."

"Now that this bridge is down, how can we get over the river?" mused Sam.

"Where do you want to go?"

"We were on our way to Hope Seminary. I suppose we can go around to the Upper Road, but it will be four or five miles out of our way."

"It ain't necessary to go that far. You go down stream about half a mile on the Craberry Road, and you can cross The Shallows."

"Isn't it too deep for an automobile?" questioned Tom.

"No, not now. It might be, though, in wet weather."

"I don't know about that," said Sam, and shook his head. "We don't want any accident in the water, Tom."

"Oh, come ahead, we can try it, anyway," returned Tom, who, in spite of the recent happenings, was as anxious as ever to get to the seminary and see Nellie.

Leaving the countryman at his self-appointed task of putting a barrier across the road—and he had said that he would also, get over to the other side of the river somehow and put a barrier there—the Rover boys swung around once again in their touring car, and headed for the side road which had been mentioned to them. Soon they reached what was known as "The Shallows," a spot where the river broadened out, and was filled with loose stones and sandbars.

By the rays from the headlights, which they now turned on to their fullest extent, the car was guided into the water. At the edge, they saw several tracks made, undoubtedly, by wagons, and one track evidently made by the anti-skid tires of an automobile.

"Well, if one auto got through, we ought to be able to make it," remarked Tom, grimly.

"Better take it on low gear," suggested his brother. "We can't see in this water, and we may go down in a hole before we know it."

Slowly and cautiously, Tom guided the machine along, trying to keep as much as possible to the high points of the various sandbars which ran in a diagonal direction to the stream itself. Once or twice they bumped over some rather large stones, and once they went into a hollow which was somewhat deeper than expected, but, with it all, they managed to keep the working parts of the car above the surface of the stream, and inside of five minutes found themselves safe and sound on the opposite shore, and headed for another side road which joined the main highway less than a quarter of a mile beyond.

"I am mighty glad we are out of that," remarked Sam, as they left the rather uneven side road and came out on the smooth highway. "I must say, I don't like autoing in the water."

"Pooh, that wasn't so bad!" replied Tom. "But it would be, I think, after a heavy storm, when the river was swollen. It must be getting late," he added. "Better speed her up a little, or we'll get to Hope just in time to say 'good-night,'" and he smiled grimly.

Fortunately for the boys, there was very little traveling that night. They met but two wagons and one automobile; and these on straight stretches of the road where there was little danger of collision. Tom was now running at thirty-five to forty miles an hour, and this was rather dangerous where the highway curved, and where what was ahead was partly hidden by, trees and bushes.

"Here we are at last!" cried Tom, presently, as they came in sight of Hope Seminary, a fine collection of buildings nestling in a pretty grove of trees. All the dormitory windows showed lights, and there was also a light in the reception parlor of the main building, for which the lads were thankful.

"Give 'em the horn, Tom," suggested Sam.

"Sure! I was only waiting to get a little closer," was the answer, and then, as the automobile turned into the seminary grounds and ran along the road leading up to the main entrance, Tom sounded the horn in a peculiar fashion, a signal which had been arranged between the boys and the girls long before.

"Tom!"

"Sam!"

The cries came from two girls dressed in white, who had been seated on a rustic bench near a small fountain. Now, as Tom brought the car to a quick stop, the girls hurried forward.

"Hello, here we are again!" sang Tom, merrily, and leaping to the ground he caught Nellie Laning by both hands. "How are you?"

"Oh, I am pretty well, Tom."

"And how are you, Grace?" came from Sam, as he, too, left the automobile.

"Oh, Sam, I am so glad you have come!" cried Grace Laning. "Nellie and I have been waiting for you."

"Well, we are glad we are here. We have had quite an adventure to-night."

"Oh, did you have a breakdown?" questioned Grace, anxiously.

"No, but we had to go to the rescue of a fellow who ran into the river."

"Oh, dear! Troubles never seem to come singly," sighed Nellie.

"What do you mean!" demanded Tom, quickly. "Is something wrong here?"

"Indeed there is, Tom!" answered Grace. And then, with a look at her older sister, who had turned her face away, she continued: "I think it is a shame! If it was not that it would make it look as if Nellie were guilty, we would pack up at once and leave this place."

"Why, what do you mean?" came from both of the Rovers.

"Oh, Grace, perhaps you had better not tell them," cried Nellie, with almost a sob.

"Nellie!" And now Tom caught the girl tightly in his arms. "What has happened?"

"I—I—can't tell!" sobbed the girl. "Grace will tell you."

"I don't suppose it is necessary to go into all the details," said Grace, "but the long and short of it is, that Nellie is suspected of stealing a four-hundred-dollar diamond ring."

"What!" ejaculated Tom.

"It was this way, Tom," pursued Grace. "One of the teachers here, a Miss Harrow, who assists the seminary management by keeping some of the books, had a diamond ring said to be worth four hundred dollars placed in her possession by a Miss Parsons, another teacher. It seems that Miss Parsons had an eccentric old aunt, who wished to give the seminary some money, and so turned over the ring, to be converted into cash. This ring Miss Harrow left on her desk in the office. Nellie went into the office to see the teacher, but finding no one there, came away. Then Miss Harrow came back a few minutes later, and found the diamond ring gone. She at once made inquiries, but as she could find nobody who had been in the once after Nellie had left, she called Nellie in and wanted her to tell what had become of the piece of jewelry."

CHAPTER IV.
A FOUR-HUNDRED-DOLLAR RING

"Did you see this ring, Nellie?" questioned Tom, after a painful pause.

"Why, yes, it was lying in the middle of a flat-top desk," responded the girl, wiping her eyes with her handkerchief.

"Didn't somebody go into the office after you were there?"

"I don't know, Tom. In fact, nobody seems to know."

"I was in the office with another girl about five minutes before Nellie went there," came from Grace. "I saw the ring there, too, and I thought it was very foolish to leave it so exposed. Why, anybody could have run off with it."

"It certainly was careless," put in Sam.

"Miss Harrow said she was on the point of putting it in the safe when she was called by 'phone to one of the other buildings. She had a dispute to settle between some of the hired help, and she did not think of the ring until some time later. Then, so she says, she rushed back to the office to find it missing."

"Well, I think it is a shame that she accused Nellie," said Tom, stoutly and with something of a savage look in his eyes. "Nellie, if I were you, I wouldn't stand for it."

"She—she hasn't accused me, exactly," returned the suffering girl. "But she intimated that I must have taken the ring, so it's just as bad."

"What does the seminary management have to say about it?" asked Sam.

"They seem to think it lies between Nellie and the teacher," answered Grace.

"In that case, how do we know the teacher didn't take the ring herself?" broke in Tom, quickly.

"Oh, do you think that possible?" questioned Nellie, in surprise.

"It's more reasonable to think she took it than you did. Anyway, she hasn't any right to accuse you," went on Tom, bluntly.

"As I said, Tom, she hasn't accused me—that is, openly; but I knew what she thinks, and I know what she will make others think," returned Nellie. And now she showed signs of bursting into tears again. "Oh, I feel as if I must pack up and go home!"

"Don't you do it, Nellie. That would make it look as if you were guilty. You stay here and face the music." Then, as Nellie began to cry again, Tom took her in his arms and held her tightly.

"Come on!" said Sam, in a low tone of voice. "I think some people at the window are listening." And he led the way to a distant portion of the seminary grounds. After that, Grace told all she knew of the miserable affair, and Nellie related just how she had seen the diamond ring on the teacher's desk.

"Was the window open at the time?" questioned the older Rover boy.

"If I remember rightly, the window was tight shut," replied Nellie.

"Yes, it was shut when I was in the office," put in Grace. "I have been trying to think out some way by which the ring could have disappeared, but without success."

The matter was talked over for some time, and then the girls questioned the boys regarding the happening at the broken bridge. Nellie, and Grace also, wanted to know the latest news from Dick and Dora.

"So far as I know, Dora is in fine health and enjoying herself in the city," said Tom. "But Dick is having his hands full, and I rather think that, sooner or later, I'll have to pack up and go to his assistance."

"Then you'll leave Brill for good?" questioned Nellie.

"I think so. I can't be breaking in on my college course every now and then as I have been doing, and pass my examinations. More than that, I begin to believe that I was not cut out for a college man. I am like Dick; I prefer a business career rather than a professional one. It is Sam who is going to make the learned one of the family."

"Oh, come now, Tom! Don't pile it on!" pleaded the younger brother. And yet he looked greatly pleased; and Grace looked pleased, too.

"But if you leave Brill, you won't be able to get here very often, Tom," remarked Nellie, wistfully.

"That is true. But if I have to go to New York, why can't you go, too?"

"Oh, Tom!"

"Well, that is what Dora did when Dick gave up his college career. I think the folks understand——"

Just then a bell in the tower of the main seminary building began to clang loudly. At the first stroke both girls started.

"There goes the first bell!" cried Grace. "We must go."

"Oh, hang the bell!" muttered Tom, and then, as Grace ran towards the building, with Sam beside her, he once more caught Nellie by the hand.

"Now say, Nellie, don't you think——"

"Oh, Tom, I must get in before the second bell rings!" pleaded Nellie.

"Yes, but won't you promise——"

"How can I promise anything, Tom, with this affair of the missing ring——"

"Missing ring! You don't suppose for one minute that that is going to make any difference to me, do you?"

"Oh, no, Tom. I know you too well for that." And now Nellie gave him a look that thrilled him through and through. "But I think I ought to clear my name before—before I do anything else."

"All right. I suppose it has got to be as you say," returned Tom, hopelessly. "But listen! If they make any more trouble for you, promise me that you will let me know."

"All right, Tom, I will." And then, after Tom had stolen a quick kiss, Nellie hastened her steps, and a few seconds later she and her sister disappeared within the building.

"Do you know what I'd like to do, Sam?" muttered Tom, as the brothers turned away from the seminary grounds in the automobile. "I'd like to wring that Miss Harrow's neck! What right has she to accuse Nellie?"

"No right at all, Tom. But one thing is certain, the ring must be missing. I don't think that the teacher had anything to do with taking it. They don't have that sort here."

"Possibly not. At the same time, to my mind it is far more reasonable to suppose that she took it than that Nellie had anything to do with it," declared Tom, stoutly.

"If the window was closed down, it seems to me that the ring must have been taken by somebody in the building," pursued Sam, thoughtfully. "Perhaps one of the hired help did it."

"Maybe." Tom gave a long sigh. "I certainly hope they clear the matter up before long. I shall be very anxious to hear from the girls about it."

As the young collegians had received permission to be out after hours, they did not attempt to take the short cut through The Shallows on returning to Brill. Instead, they went around by another road, over a bridge that was perfectly safe.

"It's not so late, after all," remarked Sam, as they entered their room. "Perhaps I had better, finish that theme."

"Oh, finish it in the morning," returned Tom, with a yawn. "You'll feel brighter."

"All right," answered Sam, who felt sleepy himself; and a few minutes later the brothers retired.

The next morning found Sam at work on the theme long before the hour for breakfast. Tom was also up, and said he would take a walk around the grounds to raise an appetite.

"As if you needed anything of that sort," grinned Sam. "The first thing you know, you'll be eating so much that the college management will be charging you double for board."

Down on the campus, Tom ran into Songbird, and, a few minutes later, William Philander Tubbs. Songbird, as usual, had a pad and pencil in his hand.

"Composing verses, I suppose," remarked Tom. "What have you got now?"

"Oh, it isn't so very much," returned Songbird, hesitatingly. "It's a little poem I was writing about dogs."

"Dogs!" chimed in William Philander. "My gracious me! What sort of poetry can you get up about dogs? I must confess, I don't like them. Unless, of course, they are the nice little lap-dog kind."

"This isn't about a lap-dog, exactly," returned Songbird. "It's about a watchdog."

"Um! By the way, Songbird, haven't the Sandersons a new watchdog?"

"Yes." And now Songbird reddened a little.

"Well, let us have the poem, anyway. I love dogs, and some poetry about them ought to run along pretty good."

Thereupon, rather hesitatingly, Songbird held up his writing-pad and read the following:

"The sun sinks low far in the west—
    The farmer plodeth home to rest,
The watchdog, watching in the night,
    Assures him ev'ry thing is right."

"Fine!" cried Tom. "Real, dyed-in-the-wool poetry that, Songbird. Give us some more." And then the would-be poet continued:

"The sun comes up and it is morn,
    The farmer goes to plow his corn,
The watchdog, watching through the day,
    Keeps ev'ry tramp and thief away."

And be it night or be it day— —"

"The watchdog's there, and there to stay!"

continued Tom, and then on:

"The watchdog, watching in his sleep,
    Catches each flea and makes him weep!"

"Catching fleas indeed!" interrupted Songbird. "Now, Tom, I didn't have any fleas in this poem."

"But all dogs have fleas, Songbird—they own them naturally. You wouldn't deprive a poor, innocent dog of his inheritance, would you?"

"But, Tom, see here— —"

"But I wanted to say the poem couldn't be better," went on the fun-loving Rover. "Why don't you send it to some of the dog journals? They would be sure to print it."

"Dog journals?" snorted the would-be poet. "Do you think I write for such a class of publications as that?"

"Well, you might do worse," responded Tom, coolly. "Now, for a first-class journal, they ought to pay you at least a dollar a foot."

"Oh, Tom, you are the worst ever!" murmured Songbird, as he turned away. A few minutes later, Tom saw him sit down on a bench to compose verses as industriously as ever.

"I think I must be going," said William Philander, who had listened to Songbird's effort without making any comment.

"Wait a minute, my dear Billy, I want— —"

"Now, Tom, please don't call me Billy," pleaded the dudish student.

"Oh, all right, Philly. I was just going to say— —"

"Now, Tom, Philly is just as bad as Billy, if not worse. You know my name well enough."

"All right, Tubblets. If you prefer any such handle to the tub, why I— —"

"Tom, if you are going to talk that way, I'll really have to leave you, don't you know," cried William Philander. "I am not going to stand for it any longer. I have told you at least a hundred times— —"

"No, not a hundred times, not more than sixty-eight times at the most," interrupted Tom.

"Well, I've told you enough times, anyway, Tom. So if you— —"

"Don't say another word, or you'll make me weep," said Tom, and drew down his face soberly. "Why, my dear fellow, I wouldn't hurt your feelings, not for the world and a big red apple thrown in. But what I was going to say was this: Are you going to play on our baseball team this Spring? Somebody said you were going to pitch for us," and Tom looked very much in earnest.

"Me pitch for you?" queried William Philander. "Why, who told you such a story as that?"

"It's all over college, Tubbs, all over college. You must be practicing pitching in private."

"But I don't know a thing about pitching. In fact, I don't know much about baseball," pleaded the dudish student.

"Oh, come now, Tubbs—you can't fool me. Most likely you have been practicing in private, and when you come out on the diamond you will astonish everybody. Well, I am glad to know that Brill College is really to have a first-class pitcher at last. We need it if we are going to win any baseball games.

"Now, Tom, I tell you that I don't know——"

"Oh, you can't fool me, William," declared Tom, positively. "I got the information straight, and I know it is absolutely correct. You are booked as the head pitcher for Brill this season." And thus speaking, Tom turned on his heel and walked off, leaving William Philander Tubbs much perplexed.

CHAPTER V.
THREE LETTERS

A new idea had entered Tom's mind, and he lost no time in carrying it out. Meeting Bob Grimes and Stanley Browne, he drew them quickly to one side and mentioned the talk he had had with William Philander.

"Now, carry it along," he concluded. "If you do it properly, we'll have a barrel of fun out of it."

"Right you are!" returned Bob, and Stanley winked knowingly. Then Tom hurried off, to interview several others of the students, principally those who were interested in the Brill baseball nine.

Just before the bell rang for breakfast, William Philander found himself confronted by Bob, who shook hands cordially. "This is the best news yet, William," said the baseball leader, heartily. "I have been wondering what we were going to do for a pitcher this season."

"Yes, it's all to the merry," put in Stanley, who had come up with Bob. "But tell us privately, William, are you going to depend on a straight ball and speed, or are you going to give them some curves and fadeaways?"

"Now, see here!" spluttered the dudish student. "I am not a baseball pitcher, and I want you to——"

"Oh, William, don't try that game on us! '" burst out Stanley. "We know that you have been practicing pitching for the past two months; that you took lessons from one of the greatest ball twirlers in the Western League. Of course, we understand that you wanted to surprise us; and I must confess, it is a surprise."

"But a mighty agreeable one," came from Spud, who had joined the crowd, while Tom hovered behind William Philander, grinning broadly over what was taking place. "Brill has wanted a really great pitcher for years. Of course, we have won some victories with ordinary pitchers, but the moment I heard that you had taken to twirling the sphere, I said to all my friends; 'This is the year that Brill is going to come out on top.' My dear Tubbs, I think we ought to get down on our knees, and thank you for doing this much for our college. I am sure the board of directors, when they hear of this, will certainly give you a vote of thanks, because success in baseball and other athletic sports is what makes a college in these days. And you are taking up the sport in such a thoroughly systematic manner."

"Oh, my dear fellow!" pleaded William Philander, frantically. "This is all some dreadful mistake, don't you know. How it came about, I can't imagine, but I haven't— —"

"It's no use, fellows. He simply won't acknowledge it yet," broke in another student.

"We'll have to wait until he comes out on the diamond in his new uniform," added still another.

"Anyway, William, you might tell us whether you are going to use a straight ball or a curve and the fadeaway," pleaded Stanley.

"He is going to keep that a secret, so as to fool our opponents," broke in Tom. "And he'll fool them all right enough, you can depend on W. P. Tubbs every time."

"Three cheers for W. P.!" cried Spud. "Now, then, boys, altogether: W. P., the champion pitcher of Brill College!"

A cheer and a yell rent the air, and brought a great number of other students to that part of the campus. In a twinkling, William Philander was completely surrounded.

"What's it all about?"

"Is it a fight?"

"Who are they cheering?"

"It's all about Mr. W. P. Tubbs, Esq.," cried Tom, loudly. "Our new, double back-action, warranted, baseball twirler; the man who is going to shoot 'em over the plate in such a marvelous fashion that our rivals will go down and out in one, two, three order."

At his announcement, a great hubbub arose on all sides.

"Tubbs! is he a baseball pitcher?"

"I didn't know he knew a thing about baseball."

"That dude launching a fadeaway? That gets me!"

"Where did he learn to pitch?"

"Who put him on the team?"

"Say, Tubbs, explain this, won't you?" This last remark came from four students in unison.

"You let me out of this!" cried the dudish student in despair. "It's all some horrid joke! I am not going to pitch! I don't know anything about pitching! I don't know hardly anything about baseball! I don't want to play! Why, when a fellow falls down running around the bases, he is apt to get all dirty! You let me out of this!" And so speaking, William Philander Tubbs pushed his way out of the crowd, and fairly ran for the nearest of the school buildings.

"I guess that will hold W. P. for a while," was Tom's comment, as the tall student vanished.

"Good joke, Tom!" returned Bob.

"What's the matter with keeping it up?" added Spud. "Don't let him know the truth. Maybe some day we can drag him out on the diamond."

"All right," answered Tom. "I'll do it;" and then, as the bell rang for breakfast, all of the students hurried inside.

Some days passed, and during that time the Rover boys waited anxiously for some news from their brother Dick, and also for word from Hope Seminary. In the meantime, the lads had settled down to the usual grind of college life, and were doing as well as could be expected considering the interruptions their studies had suffered.

The Rover boys had already learned that the bridge across the Paxton River had been repaired. The automobile, which had gone into the stream, had been found intact, only needing some cleaning to make it once more useable. It had been taken to the hotel garage. The young man, who had been thrown into the stream at the time, was still in bed under the doctor's care. Evidently, the shock to his system had been more severe than had been at first supposed.

"Letters at last!" cried Tom, on the third morning, as he came in, holding up several epistles. One was from Grace, another from Nellie, and still a third from Dick.

As might have been expected, the boys opened the letters from the girls first.

"Nothing new in this," remarked Tom, somewhat disappointedly, after having read what Nellie had written. "She says that the diamond ring has not yet been found, and that everything is at a standstill concerning it."

"Grace says practically the same thing," returned Sam. "She adds that Nellie is very much downcast, and she thinks that, while her friends all stand by her, some of the girls are giving her the cold shoulder."

"It's an outrage! Oh, Sam, I wish I could do something!" And unable to control his feelings, Tom clenched his hands and began to pace the floor.

"It certainly is the meanest thing I ever heard of, Tom. But I don't see what we can do. In fact, I don't see what anybody can do. The seminary management must have made a thorough investigation, and if they haven't discovered anything, I don't see how an outsider can solve the mystery."

"Maybe they ought to shadow some of the hired help, or something like that."

"They may be doing that, Tom. They certainly won't let a four-hundred-dollar ring get away from them without making the biggest kind of an effort to find out where it went. But open that letter from Dick, and see what he has to say."

The communication was torn open, and Tom glanced over it hastily.

"Here's a surprise, Sam," he cried. "Well, what do you know about this!" And he read as follows:

"I have something of a surprise for you. In coming to a settlement with Pelter, Japson & Company, they notified me that they were going out of business in New York City. Pelter claims that our exposing the firm practically ruined them, and at the present time there is still due father a matter of about fifteen hundred dollars, which they seem unable to pay. Both Pelter and Japson have offered to turn over to us the entire contents of their offices in Wall Street, along with their lease. I don't think the outfit is worth the fifteen hundred dollars, but when you can't get all that is coming to you, the next best thing is to take what you can get. I am writing to father about this, and if he agrees with me, I shall take the lease of the offices, and also the outfit, which includes several desks, chairs, a safe and a filing cabinet. Pelter says the outfit was new two years ago, so that it is in quite good condition.

"Dora sends her best regards. As you know, we are now installed in our suite at the Outlook Hotel, and she spends quite some of her time shopping and looking around the city. I have gone out with her a few times, but spend most of my time in straightening out these financial matters, and in taking care of father's other investments. Mr. Powell, the lawyer, is assisting me to unravel the tangle, but it is hard work, and I often wish that one or both of you were here to help me. Remember me to all the boys and likewise to Grace and Nellie.

"By the way, I understand that Josiah Crabtree is soon to leave the hospital. His leg was so badly broken that he will have to walk with either a crutch or a couple of canes. In one way, I feel sorry for the old fellow, but he brought the accident on himself. What a shame that a man with his education couldn't have remained honest and straightforward.

"As I said above, Pelter, Japson & Company, are going to give up business here. Just the same, I don't like Pelter's actions at all. I think he is a bad one through and through—much worse than Japson—who is more weak than wicked. I am going to keep my eyes open whenever Pelter is around."

Both boys read this communication from Dick with deep interest. Then Sam read the letter a second time and looked thoughtfully at Tom.

"I don't think Dick is having any easy time of it," was his sober comment.

"Just what I have been thinking all along, Sam. When Dick says he wishes he had one or both of us with him, he means it. Just as soon as the college term comes to a close, I am going to New York."

"Well, I'll go with you," returned Sam. "I did think we might go on some kind of an outing during July and August, but it wouldn't be fair to take the time off and leave Dick at the grind alone."

"Of course, I think we ought to go home first," continued Tom, after a pause. "The folks will want to see us, and, besides, we will want to talk matters over with dad, and also with Uncle Randolph. They may want to tell us something about the business."

"Do you think that Uncle Randolph had much money invested with father?"

"I don't know exactly what to think, Sam. Uncle Randolph is very peculiar, and since father has been sick again, he has not wanted to talk matters over very much. We will have to be careful of what we say when we get home. It won't do, so the doctor said, to excite him too much."

"Oh, I know that as well as you do. In fact, it might be best not to mention business to dad at all. You must remember that this is the third breakdown he has had since we came to Brill, and another such turn might prove serious."

"Oh, don't talk like that! It makes me shiver to think of it. What in the world would we do if anything happened to poor, dear dad!"

"If only Uncle Randolph was more of a business man, he might go to New York and help Dick; but you know how he is all wrapped up in what he calls 'scientific farming.' Of course, it doesn't amount to a hill of beans, but he thinks it does, and he spends a great deal of money on it that might be put to better usage."

"Well, it's his own money, you must remember, and he has a right to do what he pleases with it. But for gracious sake! don't get him to go to New York. It would only mix up matters worse than ever. Dick would not only have to take care of the business, but he would also have to take care of Uncle Randolph. Besides, it wouldn't be fair to leave Aunt Martha to look after dad, alone." And there, for the time being, the talk on personal matters came to an end.

CHAPTER VI.
BASEBALL TALK

With so many other affairs to claim our attention, I have purposely avoided going into the details of the baseball season at Brill that year. As my old readers know, the college had a baseball nine and a football eleven, and both had, at various times, done well at one sport or the other.

This particular year, baseball matters had not gone as well as had been expected. In the first place, several of the best players on the nine had graduated the year before and left the college. Then had come a long wet spell, during which time only some indoor practice in the gymnasium could be attempted. Thus, at the opening of the season, the nine possessed four players who had hitherto played only on the scrub, and the whole team lacked the practice that was essential to success. The most serious loss was in the battery, both the pitcher and catcher of the year previous having left the college. Bob Grimes, who played at shortstop, was the captain, and after a good many tryouts, he had put Spud Jackson in as catcher. For pitcher, there were three candidates: a lad named Bill Harney, who was a tall junior; a much smaller chap who had come from Yale, named Dare Phelps; and Tom, who had been pushed forward by a number of his friends. Tom had thought to pay strict attention to his studies for the remainder of the term, but finally agreed to accept the position if it was offered to him.

"I think you are going to make it, Tom," said Songbird one day after Tom had been pitching on the regular team against Bill Harney, who had been pitching on the scrub. Tom had managed to hold the scrub down to three hits, while Harney had allowed fourteen hits, one of which had been turned by the batter into a home run.

"Oh, I don't know about that," replied Tom. "Harney isn't so bad. He had a little ill luck to-day, that's all. And then, don't forget Phelps."

"I'm not forgetting either of them. Just the same, I think you are going to make the nine."

The next day, Tom was put in as pitcher on the scrub, while Dare Phelps occupied the box for the regular nine. For the first six innings, it was a nip-and-tuck battle between the two pitchers. But from that time on, Dare Phelps seemed to go to pieces, while Tom struck out man after man. As a result, the score at the end of the game stood 4 to 10 in favor of the scrub.

"Tom, I think that settles it!" cried his brother, as he rushed up and took the other by the shoulder. "You certainly held them down in great shape."

"And say, didn't the scrub bang Phelps all over the diamond!" broke in another student. "My, he must feel pretty sore!" And evidently this was true, because a minute later Dare Phelps left the diamond and disappeared from view. Nearly everybody in the college had watched the games between the scrub and the regular nine; and that night the concensus of opinion seemed to be that Tom ought to pitch for the regular team.

"You'll have to do it, Tom," said Bob Grimes, when he called on the older Rover in the morning. "Phelps acknowledges that you are a better pitcher than he is, and I think Bill Harney will have to do the same."

"Better wait and see how I pitch in one of the regular games," returned Tom, modestly. "For all you know, I may go to pieces."

"Nonsense, Tom! I know you too well for that," and Bob grinned broadly. "We'll show Roxley College this year what we can do."

Every year there were two contests between Brill and Roxley, a rival college located some miles away. One contest was at baseball, and the other football. During the past Fall, Roxley had suffered its second defeat on the gridiron at the hands of Brill. But the Spring previous, its baseball nine had literally "wiped up the diamond" with Brill by a score of 6 to 0. My, readers can, therefore, well imagine how anxious the baseball management was to win the game scheduled to come off in about a week.

Since returning to college from his trip to New York, and then the longer trip to Alaska, Sam had given almost his entire time to his studies. He was quite a baseball player, but he felt that to play on the regular team would take too much of his time.

"If you are going to leave college this June, it won't make so much difference whether you pass with flying colors or not, Tom," he said. "But if I am to return in the Fall, I want to make sure that I am not going to do so under conditions."

"But, Sam, I don't see why you can't play a game or two," persisted Tom. "It doesn't seem natural for you to keep out of it altogether."

"Well, I have played some on the scrub."

"Oh, I know, but that isn't like going in for the regular thing. You could be on the regular team if you really wanted to."

This matter was talked over several times, but Sam refused to be entirely persuaded. He, however, finally agreed to go on the bench as a substitute, provided Bob would not ask him to play any inside position. By a toss-up, it had been decided that the game should take place on the Roxley grounds. As a consequence, the boys of Brill and their friends would have to go to the other college either by train from Ashton, or in automobiles or some other kinds of conveyances.

"Of course, we'll take the girls, Tom," said Sam, in talking the matter over. "We can go over to Hope in the auto for them, and I think it would be nice if we took Songbird along and stopped at the Sanderson cottage for Minnie."

"All right, that suits me," replied Tom, "Let us ask Songbird about it."

Of course the would-be poet was delighted, and he at once sent a note to Minnie, asking her to be ready when the auto arrived. The girls at Hope were communicated with over the telephone.

"I'm afraid it's going to rain," said Spud, on the evening before the great game was to take place. And Spud was right. By nine o'clock it was raining steadily.

"Just our confounded luck!" muttered Songbird, as he paced up and down the room which he and half a dozen others were occupying. "Now, I suppose that game and our nice auto ride will be all knocked in the head."

"Don't worry so early," returned Sam, cheerfully. "I don't think this is anything more than a shower, and we need that to lay the dust." Sam proved to be right, for before some of the boys retired, the rain had stopped coming down, and one by one the stars began to appear. In the morning, the sun came up as bright as ever, and by ten o'clock the ground was as dry as any one could wish. The day was a Saturday, and, of course, a holiday both at Brill and Roxley. By eleven o'clock, a carryall had taken a large number of the students to Ashton, where they were to take a special train for Roxley. All of the automobiles at Brill were in use, and with them all of the turnouts that could be hired in the vicinity.

"No time to spare!" sang out Tom, as he ran the automobile up to the college steps.

"I am ready," said Sam, who had a dresssuit case with Tom's uniform and his own in it.

"Where is Songbird?"

"I don't know, I thought he was with you."

"Here I am!" came the cry, and the would-be poet of the college came rushing across the campus. He was dressed in his very best suit, and wore a rose in his buttonhole.

"Wait! I almost forgot the horns!" cried Sam, and he darted back into the building, to reappear a few seconds later with several long tin horns. Into the automobile piled the boys, and then, with a loud sounding of the horn, Tom turned on the power, and the machine started off in the direction of Hope, soon reaching the spot where the automobile had gone into the river.

"That poor chap didn't hurt his machine much, so I have heard," remarked Sam, as they bowled along over the bridge. "But, I think it might have been better if he had come out of it scott free, and the auto had gone to pieces."

"We ought to call on him, Sam," returned Tom. "I would like to find out whether or not he is related to Jesse Pelter."

"Oh, don't bother about that to-day. Let your, mind rest on the game—and the girls," and Sam grinned faintly.

The run to the seminary did not take long. The Laning girls stood waiting on the porch, and once they were in the car, the machine was headed in the direction of the Sanderson cottage.

Nellie occupied the front seat with Tom, while Sam was in the tonneau with Grace and Songbird. The younger girl was in her usual happy mood, but Nellie's face showed worriment.

"Have you heard anything more about the missing ring?" questioned Tom, while on the way to the Sanderson farmhouse.

"Not a thing, Tom," answered Nellie, soberly.

"Of course they have questioned the hired help?"

"Yes. And they have also questioned a number of the teachers and the students."

"Has Miss Harrow said anything more about it to you?"

"No, but every time we meet, she gives me such a cold look that it fairly makes me shiver. Oh, Tom, sometimes I don't know how I am going to stand it!" And now the girl showed signs of breaking down.

"There, there! Don't think about it any more, Nellie—at least, for to-day. Think of the jolly good time we are going to have and how we are going to defeat Roxley."

"Do you think Brill will win, Tom? I heard some of the girls at Hope say that they were sure Roxley would come out ahead. They said they have an unusually strong nine this year, and that they have already won some games from the strongest nines around here."

"Well, that is true. Nevertheless, we hope to come out ahead."

"Sure we'll come out ahead!" cried Songbird. "With Tom in the box it's a cinch."

"Just what I say," broke in Sam. "Tom has got some curves that are bound to fool them."

In order to make time, Tom had put on nearly all the speed of which the car was capable, and in a short while they came in sight of the Sanderson farm. Mr. Sanderson was at work in an apple orchard near by, and waved his hand to them as the machine drew up to the horse-block.

"Better come along," sang out Sam, gaily.

"I wouldn't mind a-seein' the game," returned the old farmer. "But I've promised to pick these early apples and ship 'em. I wish you boys luck." And then he brought over a pail full of apples, and dumped them in the tonneau of the car. Minnie, looking as fresh and sweet as ever, was on the piazza, and when the car stopped she hurried down the garden walk. Songbird leaped out and helped her in beside Grace, shaking hands at the same time.

"Good gracious, Pa! how could you do so?" said Minnie, reproachfully, as she stepped between the apples.

"Oh, I thought as how ye might git hungry on th' way," returned Mr. Sanderson, with a broad grin. "If ye don't want to eat them, you feed your hosses on 'em." And he laughed at his little' joke.

"We'll eat them fast enough don't worry," cried Sam, and then, with a toot of the horn, the automobile proceeded on its way to Roxley.

CHAPTER VII.
THE GREAT BASEBALL GAME

"Some crowd, this!"

"Well, I should say so! Say, this is the biggest crowd we ever had at any game."

"And look at the new grandstand, all decked out in flags and banners!"

"And look at the automobiles! We'll have to hurry up, or all the parking space will be gone."

"Hurrah, Brill! Come down here to see us defeat you, eh?" And a merry looking student, wearing the colors of Roxley on his cap, and waving a Roxley banner in his hand, grinned broadly at Tom and the others.

"No, we came to bury you," retorted Sam. "It's all over but the shouting." And then he took up one of the horns he had brought, and sounded it loudly.

"Better let me take the car to the other end of the grounds," suggested Songbird. "You fellows will want to get into your uniforms and into practice."

"Oh, we want to get good seats for the girls first," broke in Tom. "It won't take long to park the machine."

In a moment more, they found themselves in a perfect jam of touring cars, motor cycles, and carriages. Finding a suitable spot, Tom brought the touring car to a standstill, turned off the power, and placed the starting plug in his pocket. Then the entire party made its way as rapidly as possible to the grandstand, one-half of which had been reserved for the students of Brill and their friends. Here Songbird took charge of matters.

"Just leave it all to me," he said. "You fellows go in and win."

"Yes, you must win, by all means, Tom!" cried Nellie. "Just remember that I've got my eye on you."

"Yes, we all want you to win," came from Minnie Sanderson. "I am going to root—isn't that the right word?—for all I know how."

"That's the word!" cried Sam. "I declare, before you get through, you'll be a regular baseball fan!" And at this sally there was a general laugh.

Tom and Sam would have liked it had they been able to stay with the girls longer, but the other members of the team were already in the dressing room, donning their uniforms, and thither the Rovers made their way. A short while later, the word was passed around, and the Brill team marched out on the grounds for practice; even Sam, as a substitute, taking part. Evidently, the outsiders living in that vicinity were of the opinion that the game would be well worth seeing, for long after the grandstand and the bleachers were filled, the crowd kept coming in the several gates.

"My, but this is going to be the banner game so far as attendance goes," remarked Sam to Bob.

"Yes, and it will bring us in a neat bit of money," returned the Brill captain.

"How are they going to divide this year?"

"One-third and two-thirds," returned Bob; meaning thereby that the winning team would take two-thirds of the receipts, and the losing team the remaining third. This money, of course, did not go to the individual players, but was put into the general athletic fund of each college.

Roxley won the toss, and as a consequence, Brill went to bat first. As the first man took his position, there were cries of all sorts, mingled with the tooting of many horns and the sounds of numerous rattles.

"Now then, Brill, show 'em what you can do!"

"Knock a home run first thing!"

"Don't let 'em see first, Roxley! Kill 'em at the plate!"

The Roxley pitcher took his position, wound up; and the ball came in quickly.

"Ball one."

"That's right! Make him give you a good one."

Again the ball came in, and this time, as it was a fairly good one, the batter swung for it, and missed.

"Strike one."

"That's the talk, give him another like that, Carson!"

Again the ball came whizzing over the plate. The batsman struck it fairly, and it sailed down toward second base. The runner was off like a shot, but it availed him nothing. The second baseman caught the fly with ease.

"Hurray! One down! Now for the other two!"

The second man at the bat went out in one-two-three order. Then the third player up knocked a short fly to first.

"Three out. That's the way to do it, Roxley!"

"Now, for a few runs!"

It must be confessed that Tom was a trifle nervous when he took the ball and walked down to the box. The eyes of over twelve hundred spectators were on him, and those included the eyes of the girl he thought the dearest in all the world. He gave a short sigh, and then suddenly braced up. "I've got to do it," he muttered to himself. "I've simply got to!"

As was to be expected, Roxley had its best batters on the top of the list. The first fellow to face Tom was a hitter well-known for his prowess. As Tom had heard that this man loved a low ball, he purposely sent in the sphere rather high.

"One ball."

"That's right, Clink! Make him give you what you want."

The next ball was intended for an out-curve, but, somehow, Tom missed it, and it came in fairly over the plate. Crack! The bat connected with it, and away the sphere sailed to center field.

"Run, run!" The cry echoed from all sides, and, almost in a twinkling, Clink was down to first, and racing for second. Then, feeling that he had time to go further, he bounded onward, and slid safely to third.

"That's the way to do it! Look, a three-bagger!"

"Hurray! We've got them on the run; keep it up, boys!" And then the air was rent with the noise of horns and rattles.

"Steady, Tom, steady," whispered Bob, as he walked toward the pitcher. "Don't let them rattle you; take your time."

"They are not going to rattle me," returned Tom, and set his teeth hard. He faced the new batsman, and then, of a sudden, twirled around and sent the ball whizzing to third.

"Look out! look out!" yelled the coach at third, and Clink dropped and grabbed the sack just in the nick of time. Then Tom went for the batter. One strike was called, and then two balls, and then another strike, and a ball.

"Don't walk him, Tom, whatever you do," said Spud, as he came down to consult with the pitcher.

"All right. What do you think I ought to give him?"

"Try him on an in-shoot."

Once again, Tom sent the ball over to third, almost catching Clink napping as before. Then, the instant he had the sphere once more in his possession, he sent it swiftly in over the plate.

"Three strikes! Batter out!"

"Good for you, Rover! That's the way to do it!"

"Now kill the other two, Tom!"

But to "kill the other two" was not so easy. The next man went out on a pop fly to third, which held Clink where he was. Following that came a safe hit which took the batter to first and allowed Clink to slide in with the first run. For the moment pandemonium seemed to break loose. The Roxley cohorts cheered wildly and sounded their horns and rattles. Brill, of course, had nothing to say.

"Oh, Songbird, they got in a run!" remarked Nellie, much dismayed.

"Well, the game is young yet," returned the Brill student. Nevertheless, he felt much crestfallen to think that Roxley had scored first.

With one run in, and a man on first, Roxley went to the bat with more confidence than ever. But it availed nothing, for Tom finished the inning with the Roxley runner getting no further than second.

"Now, boys, we've got to do something," said the Brill captain, when the nine came in. "Two runs at least, and three if we can possibly get them."

"What's the matter with half a dozen, while we are at it?" laughed the second baseman.

"All right. As many as you please," returned Bob.

But it was not to be. With all her efforts, Brill managed, during this inning, to get no further than third. Tom came in for a try at the bat, but the best he could do was to send up a little pop fly that the rival pitcher gathered in with ease. Then Roxley came in once more, and added another run to her credit.

"Hurrah for Roxley! That makes it two to nothing!"

There were looks of grim determination on the faces of the Brill players when they went to the plate for the third time. The first man up was struck out, but the second sent a clean drive to left field that was good for two bases. Then came a sacrifice hit by Spud, that advanced the runner to third, and on another one-base hit, this run came in amid a wild cheering by the Brill followers.

"Hurrah! One run in! Now, boys, you've broken the ice, keep it up!" And then the horns and rattles of the Brillites sounded as loudly as had those of the Roxley followers a short while before.

But, alas! for the hopes of our friends! The only other run made that inning was a third by Roxley!

During the fourth inning, Roxley added another run to her score. Brill did nothing, so that the score now stood 4 to 1 in favor of Roxley. The fifth inning was a stand-off, neither side scoring. Then came the sixth, in which Frank Holden, the first baseman, distinguished himself by rapping out a three-bagger, coming in a few seconds later on a hit by the man following him.

"Up-hill work, and no mistake!" said the Brill captain, when the team had come in for the seventh inning.

"See here, Bob, if you think you would rather try some of the other pitchers——" began Tom.

"Nothing of the sort, old man. You are doing very well. I don't consider four runs against two any great lead. And you haven't walked as many men as their pitcher."

The seventh inning brought no change in the score. But in the eighth, Roxley added another run, bringing her total up to five.

"Looks kind of bad," said Sam, to another substitute on the bench. "Five to two, and the ninth inning. We've got to play some if we want to beat them."

"Sam, I want you!" cried Bob, coming up. "Felder has twisted his foot, and you will have to take his place in left field."

"Am I to bat in his place?" questioned the youngest Rover.

"Yes."

"All right. I'll do the best I can."

There was silence around the grounds when the Brill team came to the bat. With the score 5 to 2 in favor of Roxley, it looked rather dubious for the visitors. Some of the onlookers, thinking the game practically over, started towards the gates, and the carriages and automobiles. The first man up was the captain, and he walked to the plate with a "do or die" look on his face.

"Now, Bob, lam it out for all you are worth!" shouted one of his admirers.

The first ball sent in was too low, and Bob let it pass him; but the second was just where he wanted it. The bat swung around like lightning, and, following a loud crack, the sphere sailed off towards left field.

"Run, Bob, run!" yelled a great number of his friends, and the captain let go all the speed that was in him. When the ball finally reached the diamond, it found Bob safe on third.

"That's the way to open up! Now, then, bring him in!"

This was not so easy. The batter up tried a sacrifice hit, but the ball rolled down well towards the pitcher, who landed it at first in a twinkling. Bob attempted to get home, but then thought better of it, and slid back to third. The next batter up was Sam. He had with him his favorite ash stick, and, as he stepped behind the plate, he gritted his teeth and eyed the pitcher closely.

Carson had been practicing on what he called a fadeaway ball, and now he thought this would be just the right thing to offer Sam. He wound up with a great flourish, and sent the sphere in.

Sam was on his guard, and calculated just right. His bat came around in a clean sweep, and on the instant the ball was flying down towards deep center.

"My! look at that!"

"Run, Rover, run!"

No sooner had the ball connected with the bat, than Bob, at third, was on his way home. He reached the plate before Sam touched first. Then Sam, skirting the initial bag, tore straight for second, and then for third. In the meantime, the fielder was still running after the ball. As Sam started for home, the fielder managed to capture the sphere, and threw it with all his skill to the second baseman.

"Run, Sam, run!" yelled Tom, fairly dancing up and down in his anxiety. "Leg it, old man, leg it!"

And certainly Sam did "leg it" as he never had before. Straight for the home plate he came, and slid in amid a cloud of dust, just before the ball came up from the field.

"Hurrah! hurrah! a home run!"

"Now, boys, we've started the ball rolling," cried out Bob. "Remember, only one more run ties the score."

CHAPTER VIII.
HOW THE GAME ENDED

The next batter up was plainly nervous. He had two strikes called on him, and then he knocked a small foul, which was quickly gathered in by the third baseman. Then Tom came to the bat, and was lucky enough to make a clean one-base hit. After that, came several base hits in rapid succession. These brought in not only Tom, but also the man behind him. Then came a bad fumble on the part of the Roxley shortstop, and, as a result, another run was put up to the credit of Brill.

"Seven runs. That's going some!"

"I guess this is Brill's game, after all."

"Make it a round dozen while you're at it, boys."

But this was not to be. The hits for Brill had evidently come to an end, and the side retired with seven runs to its credit.

"Now, Tom, hold them down if you possibly can," said Bob, as his team took the field.

"I'll do my level best, Bob," was the reply.

With the score five to seven against them, Roxley put in a pinch hitter by the name of Bixby. This player certainly made good, getting a three-base hit with apparent ease. Then followed an out, and then another base hit, bringing in Bixby's run. Then followed some ragged play on the part of Bob and his second and third basemen, which put out one man, but evened up the score, 7 to 7.

With two men out, and the score a tie, it was certainly a delicate position for Tom.

"Tom, hold them! please hold them!" pleaded Bob, as he came up. "Don't let them get as far as first if you can help it."

The batter to face Tom was a fairly good one, but the young pitcher remembered that this fellow had always struck at balls which were both high and far out. Accordingly, he fed him only those which were low and well in, "One strike!"

"That's it, Tom! Keep it up!"

Again Tom wound up, and the ball shot over the plate. This time the batsman swung for it, but failed to connect.

"Strike two!"

"Good boy, Tom, that's the way to do it!"

"Be careful, Billy, make him give you just what you want!"

Once again Tom wound up, and this time sent the ball in with all the speed that was left to him. Again the bat came around.

"Strike three! Batter out!"

A wild yell arose. Here was the end of the ninth inning, and the game was a tie!

"Oh, Songbird! do you think Brill will win?" exclaimed Grace, anxiously.

"I certainly hope so. We've pulled up pretty well. We had only two runs when they had five, remember."

"Hasn't Tom pitched pretty well?" questioned Minnie.

"Sure, he has! Those Roxley fellows are great batters. More than once they have knocked a pitcher clean out of the box."

"Oh, I certainly hope Brill wins," murmured Nellie.

There was an intense silence when the tenth inning opened. Frank came to the bat first, and knocked a little one, but managed to reach first. Then, on a sacrifice hit, he advanced to second. Following that, came a wild throw by the Roxley pitcher, and Frank dusted as fast as he could for third.

"Now, Carson, hold him!" yelled a number of the Roxley followers to their pitcher. "Don't let him get in!"

Carson did his best, but with two strikes called on the batter, there came a neat little one-base hit, and, amid a wild cheering and a grand tooting of horns and sounding of rattles, Frank slid in to the home plate.

"Hurrah! hurrah! that makes the score eight to seven!"

"Keep it up, boys! You've got 'em going."

But that was the end of the run making for Brill. The next man was put out with ease, and the side retired with the score reading: Roxley—7, Brill—8.

"Now, if we can only hold them," was Spud's comment, as he glanced at Bob and then at Tom. "How about it?" he demanded, of the pitcher.

"I'll do what I can," was Tom's simple answer.

Nearly all the spectators in the grandstand and on the bleachers were now on their feet. All sorts of cries and suggestions rent the air. Amid this great hubbub, the Brill nine took their positions, Sam going down to left field as directed by Bob.

Tom was a trifle pale as he faced the first batter, but, if he was nervous, the Roxley player was evidently more so. Almost before either of them knew it, two strikes had been called. Then, however, came a short hit to third, which the baseman fumbled, and the batter got safely to first.

"That's the way! Now, keep it up!"

"We only want two runs to win."

The next batter was one that Tom, fortunately, had studied closely. This man usually waited all he could in the hope of having balls called on the pitcher. As a consequence, Tom fed him several straight ones over the plate, and so quickly that two strikes were called almost before the baseman realized what was occurring. Then, as he swung at a low one, the third strike was called, and he was declared out. In the meantime, however, the runner on first had made second. Then came another out, and then a drive to second, which landed the batsman on first, but kept the man on second where he was.

"Two men on base!"

"Bring 'em in, Landy! Bang it out for all you are worth!"

"Careful, Tom, careful!" pleaded Bob; and even Spud came down to interview the pitcher.

"I'm doing all I can," returned Tom.

It must be admitted that Tom's blood was surging wildly. A miss—and the game would either become a tie or be won by Roxley.

In came the ball, and the Roxley player swung at it viciously.

"Strike one!"

"Good boy, Tom, keep it up!"

"Strike him out, old man!"

Again Tom twirled the ball and sent it in. Just the instant before it left his hand, his foot slipped, and the sphere came in, not on a curve as the young pitcher had intended, but straight. Crack! went the bat, and in a twinkling the sphere was sailing high in the air toward left field.

"Hurrah, that's the way to do it!"

"Run, everybody run!"

"Get it, Sam, get it!"

The ball was high in the air and well over Sam's head. The youngest Rover was running with might and main down left field. The eyes of all the spectators were on him. On and on, and still on, he sped, with the ball curving lower, and lower toward the field. Then, just as the sphere was coming down, Sam made a wild clutch with his left hand and caught it.

"Batter out!"

"My, what a catch!"

"Wasn't it a beauty!"

"Brill wins the game!"

Such a riot as ensued! Hats and canes were thrown up into the air, horns tooted loudly, and the noise of the rattles was incessant. The Brill students fairly danced for joy, and their friends, including the ladies, were almost equally demonstrative.

"Sam, that's the best catch I ever saw in my life!" cried Bob, as' he ran forward to grab the young left-fielder by the hand.

"It certainly was, Sam; and you pulled me out of a big hole," came from Tom. "When I saw that fellow hit the ball, I thought it was all up with us."

"Some catch, that!" broke in Spud. And all the others on the nine, and many of Sam's friends, said the same.

Of course, Roxley was tremendously disappointed at the outcome of the struggle. Nevertheless, as was usual, she cheered her opponent, and was cheered in return. Then the two teams broke and ran for the dressing rooms, and the great crowd of spectators began to slowly disappear.

"Oh, Sam, that catch was too lovely for anything!" cried Grace, when the two Rover boys had managed to break away from the rest of the team and their numerous friends, and had rejoined the girls and Songbird. "Why, do you know, I was on pins and needles when I saw that ball coming down and you running after it. I was so afraid you wouldn't get there in time!"

"Well, I just got it, and no more," returned Sam, modestly.

"He pulled me out of a hole," broke in Tom. "If it hadn't been for Sam, Roxley would have won the game."

"But you did well, Tom,—better than our other pitchers would have done," replied his brother, loyally. "Everybody says so. Why, four or five of those Roxley hitters can knock the ordinary pitcher clean out of the box."

"Believe me, there will be some celebration to-night!" vouchsafed Songbird, as his eyes lit up in expectation. "Bonfires, speeches, parades, and all that."

"Don't I wish I was a college boy, to be there!" returned Minnie, wistfully.

"Too bad! but no girls are allowed," returned Sam. "Just the same, I don't think we'll have to get back to the college very early."

It had already been arranged that the Rovers and Songbird and the three girls should go off on a little automobile trip after the game. Grace and Nellie had received permission to be absent from Hope during the supper hour, and Tom had telephoned to the hotel at Cliffwood, about twenty miles away, asking the proprietor to reserve a table for them and prepare dinner for six.

Sam was now at the wheel, and as he could handle the car as well as his brother, the run to Cliffwood did not take long. At the hotel, the young folks encountered several other parties from Brill and Hope, and the gathering was, consequently, quite a merry one. Tom had ordered flowers for the table, and also small bouquets for each of the girls.

"Oh, how perfectly lovely, Tom!" cried Nellie, on catching sight of the flowers.

"I think the gentlemen ought to have button-hole bouquets," said Grace.

"All right, I'm willing," returned Sam quickly, and thereupon some of the flowers from the larger bouquet were speedily transferred to three coat buttonholes.

It was a lively time all around, for between the courses that were served, the young folks insisted upon singing some of the Brill and Hope songs. As it happened, there were no outside guests present, so the students and their friends could do pretty much as they pleased.

"Sorry, but we've got to start back," said Tom, presently, as he looked at his watch. "Not but what I'd rather stay here than go to Brill for the celebration!" and he looked fondly at Nellie.

"What's the matter with my driving the car?" suggested Songbird, who was well able to perform that service. "You've both had a whack at it; it seems to me it's my turn now."

Both of the Rovers were willing, and a short time later, with Songbird at the wheel and Minnie beside him, and the Rovers and the Laning girls in the tonneau, the touring car left the hotel and started on the way to the Sanderson cottage and the seminary.

"What's the matter with a song?" cried Sam, as the car sped along.

"Right you are!" returned his brother. "Girls, what shall it be?"

Instead of replying, Nellie started up an old favorite at the college, sung to the tune of "Camping on the Old Camp Ground." Instantly all of the others joined in.

"Some song!" exclaimed Tom, after the first verse had come to an end. "Now then, altogether!" and he waved his hand like a band leader. The voices of the young people arose sweetly on the evening air, but hardly had they sung two lines of the second verse, when there came an unexpected interruption.

Bang! The sound came from below them. Then the touring car suddenly swerved to the side of the road. Almost as quickly Songbird threw out the clutch and applied both brakes. They came to a standstill in the middle of the roadway.

"Oh, Tom! what's the matter?" gasped Nellie "I don't know, but I'm afraid it's a blowout," was the serious reply.

CHAPTER IX.
CELEBRATING THE VICTORY,

"Oh, what luck!"

"And just when we wanted to make time, too!"

"I hope it doesn't take us long to put on another tire!"

These remarks came from the three students as they climbed down from the car to make an examination of the damage done. Sam had secured his searchlight, but this was hardly needed. One glance at the left-hand back tire told the story. They had evidently run over something sharp—perhaps a piece of glass—and there was a cut in the shoe at least three inches long. Through this, the inner tube had blown out with the report that had so startled them.

"Well, boys, everybody on the job!" cried Tom, and lost no time in stripping off his coat and donning a jumper, which he carried for use when working on the car.

"I suppose that's my fault," said Songbird, much crestfallen.

"It might have happened to any of us, Songbird," returned Sam. "Let us see how quickly we can put on another shoe and inner tube." He, too, put on a jumper, and in a few minutes the boys had the back axle of the touring car jacked up.

"You hold the light, Songbird," directed Tom. "Sam and I can do this work without any help." Then the two Rovers set to work, and in a very short time the old shoe with its inner tube had been removed. In the meantime, Songbird had brought out another inner tube, and unstrapped one of the extra shoes attached to the side of the car, and these were quickly placed over the wheel rim.

"Now, let me do my share of the pumping," insisted Songbird.

"Nothing doing on that score, Songbird!" replied Tom, quickly. "We had a new power pump installed last week. I will attach it, and then you can start up the motor."

"A power pump! Say, that beats hand pumping all to pieces."

"Indeed, it does!" broke in Sam. "I never minded putting on a new tire, but the pumping-up always came hard."

"Say, this puts me in mind of a story," came from Tom, with a grin. "Some Germans were going on an automobile tour, and a friend was bidding them good-bye. Says the friend: 'Uf you haf a blowout, be sure and haf it in de right place—at de hotel!'" And at this little joke there was a general laugh.

Five minutes more found them again on the way, and now Songbird had the large lights turned on, which made the roadway ahead as bright as day. He drove as speedily as possible, but with great care, avoiding everything that looked as if it might harm the tires.

"Oh, what a splendid time I have had!" exclaimed Minnie, as, all too soon, the Sanderson homestead was reached. Then Songbird assisted her to alight, and insisted upon accompanying her into the cottage.

"I will wager he would rather stay here than go on to Brill," remarked Tom, slyly.

"Sure thing!" returned Sam. "Wouldn't we rather remain at Hope than go to Brill?" And at this pointed remark both of the girls giggled.

Those outside waited for several minutes, and then Tom sounded the horn loudly. Soon Songbird re-appeared and took his place at the wheel, and then the automobile was turned in the direction of the seminary.

"When will we see you again?" remarked Nellie, when the touring car had been run through the grounds.

"Oh, it won't be very long," replied Tom. But as he spoke, little did he realize under what peculiar conditions they would come together again.

"If you hear anything more about that money affair, let us know at once," whispered Sam to Grace.

"I will, Sam," returned the girl; and a few minutes later the young folks bade each other a fond good-night, and the touring car turned towards Brill.

The lads were still some distance from the college grounds when they heard the sounds of horns and rattles. Then they beheld a glimmer of light down by the river bank. Soon the light brightened until it covered a goodly portion of the sky.

"Some bonfires and some noise!" was Sam's comment.

"Well, we don't defeat Roxley every day in the year," returned Tom, gaily. "Say, this suits me right down to the ground! Songbird, you ought to get up a poem in honor of the occasion."

"Perhaps I will," answered the would-be poet of the college, and then he began to murmur to himself. Evidently the poem was already beginning to shape itself in his fertile mind.

"I say, you Rovers!" came a call as the car swung into the roadway lining one side of the campus. "What's the matter with giving us a joy ride?" and one of the students came running forward, followed by several others. Two of them carried torches made of old brooms dipped in tar.

"Nothing doing to-night," returned Sam quickly, and added in a whisper to Tom: "Those fellows would wreck the car completely."

"I know it," answered the older Rover, and then he said aloud: "We have had all the run we want this evening. We are going to celebrate with the rest of the crowd down at the river." And without stopping to argue the matter, Tom ran the automobile to its garage.

"Back, safe an' sound, eh?" questioned Abner Filbury, as he came forward to take charge of the machine.

"Ab, you look out that some of the fellows don't take this car to-night," warned Tom.

"There ain't no cars goin' out less'n I've the correct orders for 'em," replied Abner. "This is the last machine in, an' I'm goin' to lock up an' stay on guard. If anybody tries to break in here against orders, they'll git a dose of buckshot in 'em." And Abner pointed grimly at a shotgun that hung on one of the walls.

"Oh, Ab, don't go in for shooting anybody!" exclaimed Sam, in alarm. "Turn the hose on them, that will be enough."

"All right, jest as you say. But they ain't goin' to git in here at these machines without permission."

Tom and Sam made a hasty visit to their room, and then hurried downstairs again and off to the waterfront. Here, several bonfires had been lit. They were composed of boxes and barrels with a large quantity of brushwood added, and one bonfire was nearly twenty feet in height.

"Here they come!" called out a student.

"Hurrah for our pitcher!"

"And the best fly catcher Brill ever saw!"

"Say, this is certainly some bonfire!" exclaimed Sam, looking at the big blaze.

"It sure is!" returned his brother. "If the wind should shift, it might prove dangerous," he added, as he watched a great mass of sparks floating across the stream and over the woods beyond.

"Oh, it's perfectly safe," came from Paul Orben, who was one of the students who had helped to pile up the combustibles.

The crowd was certainly a gay one, and the Rovers lost no time in joining in the festivities. One student had a bugle, and another had an old base drum which boasted of only one head. These two succeeded in forming a crowd of their fellow-students into marching order, and, singing gaily and tooting horns and sounding rattles, and with numerous torches flickering, the collegians tramped around the college buildings and over the campus and then back to the bonfires.

"Whoop! Hurrah!" came a sudden yell, and from one of the distant barns rushed half a dozen students, dragging behind them a buggy. On the seat, wearing an exceedingly tight jockey jacket, and likewise a jockey cap, sat old man Filbury, the general caretaker of the dormitories.

"Hurrah! Here the conquering hero comes!"

"It's a race—a race for a thousand dollars!"

"I'll bet on Filbury, every time!"

"Now, see here, gents, I don't like this at all. You lemme out o' this here kerridge," wailed the old man-of-all-work. "I ain't doin' none o' this celebratin'. I got some work to do. You let me go."

"Oh, we couldn't think of it, Filbury," cried Stanley, who was one of the students at the shafts of the carriage. "Now then, boys, together!" And along the turnout rattled, past the various bonfires.

"Speech! Speech!" came another cry. "Filbury, can't you say something about Brill and this glorious victory?"

"Never mind the victory," came from Tom. "Let him tell us about how to pass our examinations without studying."

"And how to get credit down in town without paying any bills," put in another student, who, evidently, had hard work making both ends meet.

"I tell you, I ain't a-goin' to make no speech," wailed old Filbury. "I've got work to do. You lemme go."

"Sam," whispered Tom, catching his brother, by the arm, "what's the matter with giving William Philander a ride with old Filbury?"

"Just the cheese, Tom!" returned the young Rover. "But how can we do it?"

The matter was talked over for a short minute, and Spud and Bob were called in to aid. William Philander Tubbs sat on a small packing case which had not, as yet, been fed to the flames. He was, as usual, faultlessly attired, even down to his spats.

Passing the word to those who had charge of the carriage and who were doing their best to get some fun out of old Filbury, Tom and Sam and their chums worked their way to a position behind William Philander. Then came a sudden rush, and the dudish student found himself caught up and carried bodily over to the carriage, where he was unceremoniously dumped on the seat beside the old man-of-all-work.

"My gracious me! What does this mean?" gasped the astonished William Philander. "I don't want any ride, I want you to leave me alone."

"All aboard, everybody!" sang out Tom, and gave the carriage a shove from behind. Before the dudish student could attempt to leap to the ground, the turnout was once more in motion and dashing along the campus roadway as fast as the students could pull and push it.

"Them boys is plumb crazy!" gasped old Filbury.

"Oh, I never! We shall certainly be hurt," wailed William Philander. And then, as two wheels of the turnout went over a big stone, he clutched old Filbury wildly by the shoulder. Then the carriage struck another stone, and both occupants held fast for dear life. Three times the turnout, with its terrified occupants, circled the campus. All the while William Philander and old Filbury were yelling wildly for their tormentors to stop. But now, a long rope had been hitched fast to the front axle, and fully two dozen students had hold of this, fresh ones continually taking the places of those who became tired out. As it was, Sam and Tom went around twice, and then fell out to rest.

"Say, Washer," said a student named Lamar to his close chum, "here's a chance to square up with old Filbury for the way he treated us."

"What do you mean?" asked the student named Washer.

"Let us get in the lead on the rope, and run the carriage down to the river."

"Say, that's just the cheese!" chuckled the other. "We'll do it. I think old Filbury deserves something for reporting us as he did."

On and on went the carriage, but at the turn in the roadway it was suddenly hauled over the grass and between some bushes.

"Oh, Tom, look! They are heading for the river!" cried Sam.

"All aboard!" yelled Washer. "Now then, straight ahead!" He and Lamar had headed for the water. Some of the students tried to turn to the right or the left, but others followed the leaders. In a moment more, the carriage had reached the sloping bank of the river. Then the crowd scattered, and a moment later the turnout, with a twist, struck the water and went over sideways, plunging old Filbury and William Philander into the stream.

CHAPTER X.
THE FIRE AT HOPE

"My, what a dive!"

"Everybody to the rescue!"

"Somebody get some life-preservers!"

So the cries arose as the students ran from every direction and lined the bank of the river, which, at this point, was but a few feet deep.

Old Filbury was the first to reappear, and as he stood up in water and mud that reached his waist, he shook his fist at his tormentors.

"You'll pay for this!" he cried. "I'll fix yer! I'll have yer all sent home, you'll see if I don't!"

In the meantime, William Philander had also struggled to his feet. He had lost his cap, and on the top of his head rested a mass of grass and mud. He came out of the water spluttering and shaking himself.

"I won't stand this! I'll have you all arrested!" he gasped.

"It was an accident," came from one of the students.

"It was not! It was done on purpose!"

"Sure! it was done a purpose!" roared old Filbury. "I never seen such goin's on in my life!"

"Never mind, you needed a bath, Filbury," shouted one student. And at this there was a laugh.

"I am going to report all of you," stormed William Philander. "Look at this suit, it is ruined!" and he held up the sides of his coat to view. The water and mud were dripping profusely from the garment.

"Better go down to the gym and get under a shower," suggested Spud.

"I am not. I am going to my room," retorted William Philander. And then, of a sudden, he took to his heels, burst through the crowd, and hurried toward one of the college buildings. At the same time, Filbury started to run for one of the stables.

"Say, Tom, that was rather rough," remarked Sam, after the two had disappeared.

"It sure was, Sam. I didn't think they would run the carriage into the water like that."

"It was Washer's and Lamar's fault."

"I know it. They are always out for carrying a joke to the limit. I suppose they had it in for old Filbury, and they must have had it in for Tubbs, too."

"I wonder if either of them will make a kick over the way they have been treated," put in Bob. It may be stated here, that, in the end, nothing came of the incident. Filbury stormed around a little, and so did William Philander, but, to their credit be it said, both were "sports" enough not to take their complaints to the college management.

All good times must come to an end, and by midnight the bonfires had burned themselves out, and, one by one, the students retired. The carriage was righted and taken back to the place where it belonged.

For the best part of a week after this, but little out of the ordinary occurred. With the excitement attending the close of the baseball season over, the Rovers applied themselves more diligently than ever to their studies. During that time they received notes from Grace and Nellie, stating that nothing new had developed concerning the missing four-hundred-dollar ring. They also received another letter from Dick, in which the oldest Rover boy stated that he and the lawyer had made a final settlement with Pelter, Japson & Company, and that he had heard that the brokers were about to leave New York City for good.

"By the way, Tom," said Sam, after reading the letter from Dick, "this puts me in mind: What became of that fellow we hauled out of the river?"

"The last I heard of him, he was still under the care of Doctor Havens."

"Don't you think we ought to call on him? He might want to see us."

"If he wanted that, Sam, wouldn't he send us word? Perhaps, if he is any relation to Jesse Pelter, he would rather we would keep away from him."

On the following morning a letter came addressed to Tom, and bearing the Ashton postmark. On opening the communication, he was much interested to read the following:

> Dear Mr. Rover:
>
> "I want to thank you and your brother for what you did for me. I shall never forget it. Even were I in a position to do so, I would not insult you by offering you any reward. You, perhaps, have learned my name, and maybe you are wondering if I am related to Mr. Pelter of Pelter, Japson & Company, of New York City. Mr. Pelter is my uncle, and for a number of years I made my home with him. I do not altogether like his way of doing business, and do not uphold him in his dealings with your family. But he is my uncle, and on several occasions he has assisted me very materially. For that reason, I think it is best that we do not meet.
>
> "Again thanking you, I remain
>
> > "*Yours truly,*
> >
> > > "Barton Pelter."

"I guess that explains it," said Sam, after he, too, had read the communication. "He didn't want to face us because of his relationship to Jesse Pelter."

"I am glad that he doesn't uphold Jesse Pelter in his actions, Sam."

"More than likely he would be glad to come and see us in order to thank us in person for what we did for him if it were not for his uncle, and the fact that his uncle has aided him. You know the old saying, 'You can't bite the hand that feeds you.'"

"I wonder if he is still in Ashton?"

"We might telephone to the hotel and find out."

Later on this was done, and the boys were informed over the wire that Barton Pelter had left early that morning, taking his automobile with him.

"Well, only one week more of the grind," remarked Sam one morning on arising. "Aren't you glad that the closing day is so near?"

"I think I would feel a little better if I knew how I was coming out with my examinations," returned his brother.

"But, Tom, it won't make any difference to you, if you are not coming back."

"That may be, but, just the same, I would like to get as much credit as possible while I am here."

Some of the examinations had already been held, and others were to come off within the next few days. As a consequence, the majority of the students were exceedingly busy, so that there was little time for recreation.

Since the Rovers had come to Brill, the college had been endowed with the money to build an observatory. This structure had now been completed, and the boys took great delight in visiting it and looking through the telescope which it contained. It stood on the highest hill of the grounds, so that from the top, quite a view of the surrounding country could be had.

"I am going to the observatory," said Songbird, that evening. "There is going to be some kind of a transit, and I want to see it. Either of you fellows want to come along?"

"I can't,—I've got a paper to finish up," returned Sam, who was busy at his writing table.

"I'll go. I need a little fresh air," said Tom, and reached for his cap.

At the observatory the boys found one of the professors and about a dozen students assembled. The professor was delivering something of a lecture, to which the boys listened with interest, at the same time taking turns looking through the big telescope.

"It's a wonderful sight," murmured Tom, after he had had his look. Then, followed by Songbird, he walked to a little side window which, with several others, faced in the direction of Hope Seminary.

"I suppose you would rather be at Hope than here," remarked Songbird, dryly.

"And you would rather be at the Sanderson cottage than anywhere else in the world," retorted Tom.

"It's too bad, Tom, that you are not coming back next Fall," went on Songbird, seriously. "I don't know how we are going to get along without you."

"It can't be helped. I've got to help Dick. Father is too broken down to attend to business, and I don't think it is the fair thing to put it all off on Dick's shoulders."

"Oh, I understand. But Sam will come back, won't he?"

"I think so. One of us, at least, ought to finish the course here. Dick and I are cut out for business, but I think Sam ought to go into one of the professions."

"I wish I knew what I would like to do, Tom," continued Songbird, wistfully.

"Oh, some day you will be a celebrated poet."

"I think I have got to do something more substantial than write poetry."

"Well, it all depends on the brand of poetry, Songbird." And Tom began to grin. "There are some fellows who make big money at it."

"I'd like to know who they are?" questioned the would-be poet, eagerly.

"The fellows who write up some new brand of safety razor or breakfast food."

"Tom!" And Songbird looked positively hurt. "How can you be so cruel and degrade poetry so?"

"Well, they do it, I don't. Now, if you——" Tom brought his words to a sudden stop, and commenced to stare out of the window. Far over the distant wood he had seen a strange light. Now it was increasing rapidly.

"What is it? What do you see?" demanded Songbird, as he realized that something unusual had attracted his chum's attention.

"Look there!" cried Tom, pointing with his finger. "Doesn't that look like a fire?"

"It surely does," replied the other, after a hasty inspection. "But it may be only some brush heap that a farmer is getting rid of."

"I don't know about that. Say, haven't they got a pair of field glasses here?"

"Sure!" and Songbird turned to get the article mentioned.

As rapidly as possible, Tom focused the glasses on the distant light, and took a careful look.

"Great Scott! it's a fire—and at Hope Seminary!" broke out the youth. "It looks to me as if the whole place might burn down!"

"What! A fire at Hope!" cried Songbird, and his words attracted the attention of all the others in the observatory. He, too, took a look through the glasses, and one after another the remaining students did the same.

"It certainly is a fire, and at the seminary, isn't it, Tom?"

Tom did not answer. He had already started to leave the building. Straight down the hill he tore, and then up to the building where he and the others had their rooms. He burst in on his brother like a cyclone.

"Sam, come on, quick! There is a fire at the seminary!"

The younger Rover, who was deep in his writing, looked up, startled.

"What is that you said, Tom?"

"I said, hurry up; come along; there is a fire at the seminary! The girls may be in danger! Come on, let us go there in the auto."

"Oh, Tom, are you sure of this?" And now Sam leaped up, brushing his writing to one side.

"Yes, I saw the fire from the observatory." And in as few words as possible, Tom gave his brother the particulars. He was already donning his automobile outfit. Sam followed suit, and both boys ran downstairs and to the garage.

By the time they had the touring car ready, Songbird, Stanley, Spud, and several others had joined them. The word had been passed around that there was a fire at Hope, and permission to go to the conflagration was readily granted by the college management.

"All aboard who are going!" sang out Tom, who was at the wheel, with Sam beside him. Then, after several collegians had climbed into the tonneau, away the touring car dashed over the road leading to Hope.

CHAPTER XI.
TO THE RESCUE

It was a wild ride, never to be forgotten. Tom had all the lights turned up fully, so that he might see everything that was ahead. From twenty miles per hour the speed climbed up to twenty-five, then thirty, then thirty-five, and finally forty. Over the newly-mended bridge they dashed at breakneck speed.

"Be on your guard, Tom," warned Sam.

"We've got to get there," was the grim response. "The girls may be in danger."

"Right you are! Let her go for all she is worth!"

They had been making many turns and going up-hill and down, but now came a straight stretch of several miles, and here Tom put on all the extra power the touring car could command. From forty miles an hour, they reached forty-five, and then fifty, and, at one point, the speedometer registered fifty-four.

"My gracious, Tom, don't kill us!" yelled Bob, to make himself heard above the roar of the motor, for Tom had the muffler cutout wide open.

The youth at the wheel did not answer. He was giving all his attention to the running of the car, and this was needed. Along the roadway they sped like an arrow from a bow, past trees and fences, with here and there a farmhouse or a barn. Once Tom saw a white spot in the road ahead, and threw off the power. But it was only a flying newspaper, and on he went as speedily as before.

"It's at Hope, all right!" yelled Stanley, when they slowed down at a turn of the road.

"Yes, but I don't think it is any of the main buildings," returned another student.

"I hope not," came from Sam.

There was one more small rise to climb, and then they came into full view of what was ahead. Through the trees they saw that one of the large barns, in which the fire had evidently started, was almost totally consumed. The slight wind that was blowing had carried the sparks to one of the wings of the main building, and this was now in flames at several points.

"Here comes the fire engine!" cried Bob, as the touring car swept through the seminary grounds; and he pointed down the opposite road. Along this a small engine from a nearby town was approaching, hauled by a score of men and boys. Far down another road could be heard the tooting of another engine, probably from some other town.

"We might give some of those fellows help," suggested Songbird. "What's the matter with running the car down to where they are, and hitching fast?"

"You can do it, Songbird, if you wish," returned Tom, hurriedly. "I'll join you just as soon as I find out if the girls are safe."

"And I'll go with Tom," put in Sam.

"Oh, they must be safe; the fire isn't in that part of the building," broke in Stanley. "But go ahead, you fellows, we'll take care of the machine." For he well understood how anxious the Rovers must be regarding the Laning girls.

Leaping from the touring car, Sam and Tom joined the crowd in the vicinity of the fire, composed mostly of girl students and their teachers. About a score of men and boys living in the vicinity had come up, and these, with the hired help from the institution, were doing all in their power, to subdue the flames.

"Did all of the girls get out?" asked Tom, of the first teacher he met.

"I don't know—I think so," was the answer.

The boys pushed their way along from one group of students to another, trying to catch sight of those whom they were seeking. In the meantime, Songbird and the others from Brill had taken charge of the touring car, and run it down a side road, where they hooked fast to one of the arriving fire engines, much to the relief of those who had been dragging the machine over the somewhat rough highway, and were almost exhausted.

"Oh, Sam!" The cry came from Grace, and the next instant the girl rushed up and fairly threw herself into the arms of the youngest Rover.

"Where is Nellie?" he demanded, quickly. "Is she safe?"

"Here I am!" was the call, and then Nellie came up and caught Tom by the shoulder. "Oh, isn't this dreadful!"

"It sure is, Nellie," returned Tom, as he slipped his arm around her waist. "But I am mighty glad that you are safe. Do you think everybody is out?"

"We don't know, but they ought to be out, for we had plenty of warning. The fire started in the barn, you know."

"What caused it?"

"They think one of the men must have been smoking and dropped a light in the hay. Anyway, the fire started there."

"The other fellows took the auto to help the fire engine," broke in Sam. "Here they come now," he added, as the machine came up with honking horn, and dragging one of the fire engines behind it.

"I wish we could do something to put out this blaze," came from Tom. "Sam, we must get busy."

"Right you are!"

"Oh, do be careful, both of you!" pleaded Nellie.

"Yes, don't get burnt," added Grace.

"We'll look out, don't you fear," answered Sam, and then he and Tom turned to join those at the fire engines and the hose carts.

The seminary was provided with several water towers, and from these some lines of hose had already been run to the fire. Now some additional lines of hose were laid from the fire engines, which began to take water from two cisterns. Soon the added streams showed their effect on the flames.

"Girls! girls! have any of you see Miss Harrow?" The cry came from one of the teachers, as she made her way through the crowd.

"Why, isn't she out?" asked a number.

"I don't know, I can't find her anywhere," replied the instructor.

"Was she in the building?"

"I think so. She said at supper time that she had a toothache, and was going to retire early." And thus speaking, the teacher hurried on.

"Is that the Miss Harrow who lost that four-hundred-dollar diamond ring?" asked Tom.

"Yes," replied Nellie.

"Was her room in that addition?" questioned Sam, quickly, pointing to an end of the building which was on fire in several places.

"Yes, she has the corner window, right over there," responded Grace, pointing to a spot close to where the building was in flames.

The words had scarcely left the lips of the girl, when, to the horror of those standing below, a third story window was suddenly thrown up, and the head of a woman appeared.

"Help! Help! Save me!" The cry came wildly from the woman, who was plainly terror-stricken.

"It's Miss Harrow!" cried a score of voices.

"Look! Look! The fire is on both sides of her!"

"Don't jump! Don't jump!" yelled Tom, at the top of his lungs, and he saw the teacher prepare to cast herself to the ground.

"Can't you come down by the stairs?" called out Sam, as loudly as he could. "I'm afraid to open the door! The hall is full of smoke and fire!" screamed the teacher. "Save me! Save me!"

"Haven't they got a ladder handy?" asked Tom.

"Sure, we've got a ladder—half a dozen of 'em," responded one of the men who worked around the place.

"Where is it? Show it to us, quick!" put in Sam.

"All right, this way," returned the man, and started off with Sam at his heels.

"Don't jump! don't jump! We'll help you!" cried a dozen voices to the teacher.

"We are going to get a ladder!" yelled Tom. "Stay where you are!"

And then he followed the others. The ladders were kept in a wagon shed, and it took but a few moments to bring them out. They were four in number, and of various sizes.

"I'm afraid none of 'em is long enough to reach that winder," said the man who had led the way.

"You are right," replied Tom. "But what's the matter with lashing a couple of them together? Here's a rope." And he pointed to a washline that hung on a nearby hook.

In frantic haste a dozen persons carried the ladders to the burning building. Tom followed with the rope, which he unwound on the way. Then the washline was cut, and with it two of the longest ladders were lashed together as quickly as possible. Then the combination ladder was raised against the building and set close to the window, to the sill of which Miss Harrow clung.

"I'll go up if you want me to," cried Tom, as he saw the men who belonged around the place hold back. "You steady the ladder so it doesn't slip."

"Want me to help, Tom?" asked Sam.

"No, you see that they steady the ladder." And thus speaking, Tom began to mount the rungs.

A cheer went up, but to this the youth paid no attention. In a few seconds he was at the third story window. He had to pass through considerable smoke, but as yet the flames had not reached that vicinity.

"Come, give me your hand, and step out on the ladder," cried Tom to the teacher.

"I—I can't!" gasped Miss Harrow. And now the youth saw that she was almost paralyzed from fright. She clung desperately to the window sill, evidently unable to move. Clinging to the ladder with his left hand, Tom placed his right foot on the window sill, and then he reached down and caught the teacher under the arm.

"Come, you don't want to stay here," he ordered, almost sternly, and pulled the teacher to her feet.

"Oh, oh, we'll fall! I can't do it!" were her gasped-out words.

"You've got to do it—unless you want to be burned up. Now then, if you don't want to climb down the ladder, let me carry you."

"I—I—oh—I can't move!" And with these words, the teacher sank down across the window sill.

A sudden change in the wind drove a cloud of smoke into Tom's face, and for the moment he and the teacher were hidden from the view of those below.

"Oh, look! Tom will be burned up!" screamed Nellie.

"No, he won't," returned Sam, reassuringly. "He knows what he is doing." Nevertheless, Sam was as anxious as anyone over his brother's safety.

When the smoke shifted, it was seen that Tom had hauled the teacher from the window sill and had her over his shoulder. She hung down limply, showing that she had lost consciousness. Rung by rung, the youth came down the ladder slowly with his burden.

"He's got her! He's got her!" was the glad cry, and a few seconds later Tom reached the ground, where he was immediately surrounded by the others.

"Oh, Tom, how did you do it?" cried Nellie, hysterically.

"Oh, it was not much to do—anybody could have done it," replied the youth. "Say, what am I to do with her?" he added, indicating the burden on his shoulder.

"This way, please," said the teacher who had taken charge of matters, and she led the way out on the campus and to a bench on which some of the girls had piled their fancy pillows. Here Miss Harrow was made as comfortable as possible.

By this time a third fire engine had arrived, and more streams were directed on the flames. The ladder was used by some of those at the nozzle of one of the hose lines, and by this means the fire in the wing of the main building was quickly extinguished. Nothing could be done towards saving what was left of the barn, so the firemen directed all their efforts towards keeping the conflagration from spreading.

"Well, it's about out," said Sam, a little later. "Some mess, though, believe me!"

"Oh, I am so thankful it was not worse!" murmured Grace. "Suppose it had burned down the main building!"

"Tom, you're a hero!" cried Spud, coming up.

"Nothing of the sort," retorted Tom. "Anybody could have done what I did, and you know it."

"All the same, you're the one who did it," answered Spud, admiringly.

"He certainly did," said one of the men in the crowd. "That teacher ought to be mighty thankful for what he did for her."

"I don't want her thanks," added Tom, in a low voice. "All I want her to do, is to treat Nellie fairly."

CHAPTER XII.
TOM SPEAKS HIS MIND

"Tom, Miss Harrow would like to see you."

It was an hour later, and the Rovers and the Laning girls had spent the time in watching the efforts of the others to put out the last of the fire. In the meanwhile, some of those present had gone through the addition to the main building and opened the various windows and doors, thus letting out the smoke. An examination proved that the damage done there was very slight, for which the seminary authorities were thankful.

"Wants to see me, eh?" returned Tom, musingly. "Well, I don't know whether I want to see her or not."

"You might as well go, Tom, and have it over with," suggested Sam.

"If I go, I want Nellie to go along," returned the brother. "I want her to know how I stand on this missing-ring question. By the way, how is she, all right?" continued the youth, addressing Stanley, who had brought the news that he was wanted.

"She seems to be all right, although she is very nervous. She says the reason she didn't hear the alarm and get out of the building in time, was because she had had a toothache and had taken a strong dose of medicine to quiet her nerves. Evidently the medicine put her into a sound sleep."

"How about the toothache?" asked Sam, slyly.

"Oh, that's gone now; the fire scared it away."

"Where is she?" questioned Tom.

"She is in the office with some of the other teachers."

"All right, if I've got to go, I might as well have it over with. Come along, Nellie."

"Oh, Tom, do you really think I ought to go?"

"If you won't, I won't."

"All right, then," and arm in arm, Tom and Nellie proceeded into the main building. Nellie showed the way to the office, which was located at the end of a long corridor.

"Oh, so here is the young gentleman!" cried Miss Harrow, as they entered. She was very pale, but did her best to compose herself.

"You sent for me?" returned Tom, bluntly.

"Yes. I wish to thank you for what you did for me. You are a very brave young man. Were I able to do so, I should be only too pleased to reward you liberally. But I am only a poor teacher, and — — "

"I don't want any reward, Miss Harrow. What I did anybody could have done."

"Perhaps, but — —" And now the teacher stopped short, for the first time noticing Nellie's presence. "What do you want here, Miss Laning?" she demanded, stiffly.

"I came in with Mr. Rover; he wanted me to come," was the answer. And as the teacher continued to glare at her, Nellie clung tightly to Tom's arm.

"I—I don't understand — —" stammered Miss Harrow. She was evidently much surprised.

"It's this way, Miss Harrow." answered Tom, with his usual bluntness. "Miss Laning and I have been friends for a great many years. The fact is, we hope—that is, I hope"—and now Tom looked a bit confused—"we'll be married before a great while. I have been told about the diamond ring that is missing, and I know all about how you have treated Nellie. I don't like it at all. I think you are doing her a great injustice."

"Oh!" The teacher paused abruptly and bit her lip. She glanced from Tom to Nellie and then to the others who were in the office. "I—I have not accused Miss Laning of anything," she went on, rather lamely.

"Perhaps not in so many words. But you have acted as if you felt certain she was guilty. Now, that isn't fair. She wouldn't touch anything that wasn't her own. It's a terrible thing to cast suspicion on any one. What would you say if I were to intimate you had taken the four-hundred-dollar ring?"

"Sir!" and now the teacher's face grew red. "Do you mean to insult me?"

"Not at all. But I mean to stand up for Miss Laning first, last, and all the time," replied Tom, earnestly. "I think it is an outrage to even suspect her."

For a few seconds there was an intense silence, broken only by a certain nervous movement among the others in the office. Miss Harrow bit her lip again.

"I—I am sorry if I have done Miss Laning an injustice," she said, slowly. "But the diamond ring is gone, and if the ring is not recovered, I may be held responsible for it."

"Now, my dear Miss Harrow, pray do not agitate yourself too much," broke in another of the teachers. "This is all very painful. You had better drop the matter."

"I am willing to drop it," answered Tom, before Miss Harrow could speak. "Only I want it understood that Miss Laning is to be treated with the consideration she deserves. Otherwise I may suggest to her father that she be taken away from this institution and a suit for damages be instituted."

"Oh, no! Not that! Not that!" came from Miss Harrow, and now she was plainly much frightened. "I did not accuse Miss Laning of anything, and I do not accuse her now. The ring is missing. That is all I can say about it."

"I think we had better go, Tom," whispered Nellie.

"You may leave, Miss Laning," said one of the other teachers. "We have had trouble enough for one night."

"Nellie started for the door, and Tom did the same; but before the youth could leave, Miss Harrow clutched him by the arm.

"Mr. Rover, just a word," she said in a low voice. "You did me a great service and I shall not forget it. If I have done Miss Laning an injustice, I am very sorry for it." And having thus spoken, she turned back and sank down on a couch. Tom and Nellie left and hurried to the campus, where they were speedily rejoined by Sam and Grace.

"How did you make out?" asked the younger Rover. And then Tom gave the particulars of what had occurred.

"Oh, Tom, I am glad you said what you did," cried Grace, heartily. "Now, maybe, Miss Harrow will be more careful in her actions."

"Well, I simply said what I thought," answered Tom. "They are not going to lay anything at Nellie's door if I can help it."

"Oh, Tom, but you told them that—that And Nellie grew red and could not go on.

"Well, what if I did? It's the truth, isn't it?"

"What was that?" asked Sam, curiously.

"Why, I told them that Nellie and I had been friends for years and that, sooner or later, we were going to be married."

"You did!" shrieked Grace. "Oh, Tom Rover!"

"Folks might as well know it," returned Tom. "They've got to know it when the affair comes off."

"Don't you think it's about time you boys started back for college?" came from Nellie, who was blushing deeply over the personal turn which the conversation had taken.

"Oh, there's no great rush," answered Tom, coolly.

Nevertheless, now that the conflagration was over, it was thought best by all the students to get back to the college, so a little later the crowd was rounded up by Spud and Stanley, and all climbed into the automobile. Sam ran the car, and the return was made without special incident.

"Say, Tom, if that wedding is to come off so soon, perhaps I had better be saving up for a wedding present," remarked Sam, dryly, when the two brothers were retiring for the night.

"I wouldn't advise you to start saving up just now," answered his brother. "Better get some sleep first." And then he playfully shied a pillow at Sam's head.

The next day nearly all the talk at Brill was about the fire and what Tom had done towards rescuing Miss Harrow. Many insisted upon it that Tom had enacted the part of a real hero, and he was interviewed by a local reporter, and a number of newspapers printed quite an item about the conflagration and the part he had played.

But the students had little time just now for anything outside of their final examinations. Many papers had to be prepared, and poor Tom often wondered how he would ever get through with any satisfaction, either to himself or his instructors. With Sam, the task seemed much easier, for, as Dick had once declared, Sam was "a regular bookworm," and no studies seemed to worry him in the least.

"If I get through at all, I shall be lucky," vouchsafed Tom, after passing in a particularly hard paper.

"We'll hope for the best," returned Sam.

During those days came another letter from Dick, in which he stated that he had moved into the offices vacated by Pelter, Japson & Company, and was doing his best to get everything into working order. He added that, on the request of their father, he had disposed of some stocks, and in their stead, had purchased sixty-four thousand dollars' worth of bonds.

"My, that's some bonds!" remarked Sam, on reading the letter.

"Well, bonds are usually much safer than stocks, even if they don't pay so well," answered Tom.

There was a letter from their Aunt Martha, who stated that their father did not seem to be quite as well as he had been the week previous. She added that they had called in another doctor, who had stated, after an examination, that there was no cause for alarm—that Mr. Rover must be kept quiet and not worried, and probably, he would be his old self in another month or two.

"I am glad that the college is to shut down soon," said Sam, when he and his brother were discussing this communication. "I want to see dad and make sure things are not worse than Aunt Martha pictures them."

"Exactly the way I feel about it, Sam. They may be holding back something on us just so we won't be worried."

Two days later came the final examination for, both the Rovers, and they felt much relieved. Songbird was also "out of the woods," as he expressed it, and asked them if they did not want to join him and Spud in a short row on the river.

"That suits me," cried Tom. "I want to get out into the air somewhere. I am done with classrooms forever. If it was not for the look of things, I would be turning handsprings on the campus."

"Ditto," added Sam.

"Well, come on," said Songbird. And a few minutes later the four students were down at the boathouse, getting out one of the four-oared boats.

"Say, Songbird, I should think this would put you in the rhyming fever," said Sam, as the four lads rowed out on the river.

"It does," returned the would-be poet.

"All right, turn on the verse spigot and let us have the latest effusion," cried Tom, gaily.

"The verses aren't finished yet," answered Songbird. And then resting his oar, he drew from his pocket a slip of paper and began to read:

"The term is passed,
Away we cast
  Our books and papers with great glee.
No more we'll train
Each tired brain— —"

"Instead, we'll cheer because we're free!"

concluded Tom.

"Say, that isn't half bad," broke out Songbird, enthusiastically. "I was going to put in something about flee— —"

"For gracious sake! What have fleas to do with this poetry?" interposed Tom.

"Fleas! Who said anything about fleas?" snorted Songbird. "I said 'flee,' f-l-e-e."

"Oh, I see! That's the flee that fled, not the flea who refuses to flee," went on Tom. And at this sally, the other boys laughed.

"Never mind, give us the rest of it," put in Spud.

"There isn't any 'rest'—not yet," answered the would-be poet. And then the bays resumed the row up the river.

CHAPTER XIII.
AT THE FARM

"All aboard who are going! We haven't any time to spare if you want to catch that nine-fifteen train."

"Good-bye, Tom, don't forget to write."

"Say, Spud, when you get down to the Maine coast, don't eat too many lobsters."

"And that puts me in mind, Stanley. When you reach the Grand Canyon, send me a piece of rock; I want to see how the Canyon looks."

"Say, whose baseball mitt is this anyway?" And following this question, the mitt came sailing through the air, to land on the floor of the Brill carryall.

"Please get off of my feet!" The wail came from William Philander Tubbs, who was sitting in a corner with another student partly on his lap.

"Everybody shove, and we'll be off!" cried another student, merrily.

Then came a great mixture of cries and whistles, intermingled with the tooting of horns and the sounding of rattles, in the midst of which there moved from the Brill grounds several carriages and an equal number of automobiles.

The term had come to an end, and the students were preparing to scatter. The majority were going home, but others had planned to go directly to the summer resorts where they were to spend their vacations.

"Good-bye, Brill!" sang out Tom, and, for once, his voice was a trifle husky. Now that he was leaving the college not to return, a sudden queer sensation stole over the youth. He looked at his brother, and then turned his gaze away.

"Never mind, Tom," said Sam, softly. "If I come back, as I expect, you'll have to come and visit me."

Hope Seminary was not to close until the week following, and the evening before the Rovers had visited Grace and Nellie. From them, Sam and Tom had heard news that interested them greatly. This was to the effect that Dora had invited her cousins to visit her in New York City some time during the vacation.

"That will be fine!" Tom had cried. "You come when Sam and I are there, and we'll do all we can to give you the best kind of a time." And so it had been arranged.

The boys and their friends were in the Rover touring car. This machine, it had been decided, was to remain at the college garage, in care of Abner Filbury. Abner was now driving, so that the boys were at liberty to do as they pleased.

"Let's give 'em a song," suggested Stanley, and the boys sang one college song after another, the tunes being caught up by those in the other turnouts. Thus they rolled up to the railroad station in Ashton. Then the train came in, and all the young collegians lost no time in getting aboard.

"Where are you going, my dear William Philander?" asked Tom, of the dudish student, who sat in front of him.

"I am going to Atlantic City," was the somewhat stiff reply, for William Philander had not forgotten the ducking in the river.

"Atlantic City!" exclaimed Tom. "Of course, you are not going in bathing?"

"To be sure I am! I have a brand new bathing suit ordered. It is dark blue, with pin stripes running— —"

"But see here, Billy! If you go in bathing at Atlantic City this season, you'll be chewed up."

"What do you mean?" And now the dudish student seemed interested.

"Haven't you heard about the sea serpents they have seen at Atlantic City?" demanded Tom,—"four or five of them." And he poked Sam, who sat beside him, in the ribs; and also winked at Spud, who was in the seat with William Philander.

"That's right, Tubbs," put in Sam. "Why, they say some of those sea serpents are twenty feet long."

"Oh, yes, I heard about them, too," added Spud, and now he braced himself for one of his usual yarns. "Why, they tell me that one afternoon the sea serpents came in so thickly among the bathers that it was hard for them—I mean those in bathing—to tell which was sand and which was serpents. Some of the serpents crawled up on the boardwalk, and even got into some of the stores and hotels. They had to order out the police, and then the fire department, and, finally, some of the soldiers had to come down from the rifle ranges with a Gatling gun. You never heard of such a battle! Somebody said they killed as many as ninety-seven sea serpents, and not less than three hundred got away. Why, William Philander, I wouldn't go within twenty-five miles of Atlantic City if I were you," concluded Spud.

"Oh, how ridiculous!" responded the dudish student. Nevertheless, he looked much worried. "Of course, they do report a sea serpent now and then."

"Well, you haven't got to believe it, Billy," answered Tom. "At the same time, you'll be a fine specimen of a college boy if you come back next Fall minus an arm and a leg. How on earth are you going to any of the fashionable dances in that condition?" And at this, there was a general snicker, in the midst of which William Philander arose, caught up his dresssuit case, and fled to another car.

"You can bet that will hold William Philander for awhile," remarked Sam. "He won't dare to put as much as a toe in the water at Atlantic City until he is dead sure it is safe."

"Humph! William Philander isn't one of the kind to go into the water," sniped Tom. "He belongs to the crowd that get into fancy bathing costumes, and then parades up and down on the sand, just to be admired."

It was not long before the Junction was reached, and here the Rovers had to part from a number of their friends. A fifteen-minute wait, and then their train came along. It was not more than half full, so the students had all the room they desired.

"I must say, the farm will look pretty good to me," remarked Tom, when the time came for them to collect their belongings.

"I want to see dad," returned his younger brother.

"Oh, so do I."

"Oak Run! All out for Oak Run!" It was the well-known cry of the brakeman as the train rolled into the station where the Rovers were to alight.

"Good-bye, everybody!" sang out both Sam and Tom, and, baggage in hand, they hurried to the station platform. Then the train went on its way, leaving them behind.

The boys had sent a message ahead, stating when they would arrive, and, consequently, Jack Ness, the hired man, was on hand with the family touring car.

"Back safe and sound, eh? Glad to see yer!" cried the hired man, as they approached, and he touched his cap.

"And we are glad to be back, Jack," returned Tom, and added quickly: "How is my father?"

"Oh, he's doin' as well as can be expected, Mr. Tom. The doctors say he has got to keep quiet. Your Aunt Martha said to warn both of you not to excite him."

"Is he in bed?" questioned Sam.

"Not exactly. He sits up in his easy chair. He can't do much walkin' around."

While talking, the boys had thrown their belongings into the car. Tom took the wheel, with Sam beside him, leaving the hired man to get in among the baggage. Then away they rolled, over the little bridge that spanned the river and connected the railroad station with the village of Dexter's Corners. Then, with a swerve that sent Jack Ness up against the side of the car, they struck into the country road leading to Valley Brook Farm, their home.

"Looks good, doesn't it?" remarked Sam, as they rolled along, past well-kept farms and through a pleasant stretch of woodland.

"Yes, it looks good and is good," returned Tom, with satisfaction. "The college and the city are all right enough, Sam, but I don't go back on dear old Valley Brook!"

"How the country around here has changed since the time when we moved here," went on Sam. "Do you remember those days, Tom?"

"Do I remember them? Well, I guess! And how Uncle Randolph used to be annoyed at what we did." And Tom smiled grimly.

Another turn or two, and they came in sight of the first of the farm fields. Then they reached the long lane leading to the commodious farmhouse, and Tom began to sound the automobile horn.

"There is Uncle Randolph!" cried Sam, pointing to the upper end of the lane.

"Yes, and there is Aunt Martha," added Tom, as a figure stepped out on the farmhouse piazza. Then both of the boys waved their hands vigorously.

"Back again, eh!" cried Uncle Randolph, when the car had been brought to a stop. "Glad to see you, boys," and he shook hands.

"Back again, and right side up with care!" exclaimed Tom. He made one leap up the piazza steps, and caught his aunt in his arms. "How are you, Aunt Martha? Why, I declare, you are getting younger and better looking every day!" and he kissed her heartily.

"Oh, Tom, my dear, don't smother me!" gasped the aunt. Yet she looked tremendously pleased as she gazed at him. Then Sam came in for a hug and a kiss.

"You mustn't be too boisterous," whispered Uncle Randolph, when all started to enter the house. "Remember, your father isn't as strong as he might be."

"Where is he?" both boys wanted to know.

"He is up in the wing over the dining-room," answered their aunt. "We thought that would be the nicest place for him. The window has a fine outlook, you'll remember."

"Can we go up now?" questioned Tom.

"Yes, but remember, do not say anything to excite him

"All right, we'll be careful," came from Sam. And then both lads cast aside their caps and hurried up the stairs.

Mr. Anderson Rover sat in an easy chair, attired in his dressing gown. He looked thin and pale, but his face lit up with a smile as his eyes rested on his two sons.

"Dad!" was the only word each could utter. And then they caught him by either hand, and looked at him fondly.

"I am glad to see you back, boys," said their father, in a low but clear voice. "It seems like a long while since you went away."

"And we have missed you a great deal!" broke out Sam. "It's too bad you don't feel better."

"Oh, I think I'll get over it in time," answered Mr. Rover. "But the doctors tell me I must go slow. I wouldn't mind that so much, if it wasn't for Dick. I think he ought to have some help."

"Now, don't you worry, Dad," interposed Tom, gently. "You just leave everything to us. We are both going to New York to help Dick straighten out matters, and it will be all right, I am sure." And he stroked his father's shoulder affectionately.

"But you'll have to go back to college— —" began the invalid.

"Sam is going back. I am going to help Dick, and stay with him. Now, don't say anything against it, Dad, for it is all settled," went on Tom, as his father tried to speak again. "I don't care to go back. I think Dick and I were cut out for business men. Sam is the learned member of this family."

"Well, boys, have your own way; you are old enough to know what you are doing." And now Mr. Rover sank back in the chair, for even this brief conversation had almost exhausted him.

CHAPTER XIV.
A STARTLING SCENE

"Dear old dad! Isn't it awful to see him propped up in that chair, unable to leave his room!"

"You are right, Sam. And yet it might be worse—he might be confined to his bed. I hope we didn't excite him too much."

"He was very much surprised at your determination to give up Brill, and join Dick. I guess he was afraid Dick would have to shoulder the business alone. And by the way, Tom," went on the youngest Rover, earnestly, "somehow it doesn't seem just right to me that I should put all this work off on you and Dick."

"Now, don't let that bother you, Sam. You can go to New York with me this Summer, and then you go back to college, and come out at the head of the class. That will surely please us all."

This conversation took place while the two boys were retiring for the night. They had not remained very long with their father, fearing to excite him too much. Aunt Martha had, as usual, had a very fine repast prepared for them, and to this, it is perhaps needless to state, the youths did full justice.

"It's a grand good thing that we have Aleck Pop with us," went on Sam, referring to the colored man, who, in years gone by, had been a waiter at Putnam Hall, but who was now firmly established as a member of the Rover household. "Aunt Martha says he waits on dad, hand and foot; morning, noon and night."

"Well, Aleck ought to be willing to do something for this family in return for all we have done for him," answered Tom.

Despite the excitement of the day, the two boys slept soundly. But they were up at an early hour, and, after breakfast, took a walk around the farm in company with their Uncle Randolph, who wished to show them the various improvements he had made.

"We have a new corncrib and a new root hovel," said their uncle, as they walked around. "And next week we are going to start on a new pigsty."

"Going to have one of those new up-to-date, clean ones, I suppose?" returned Sam.

"Yes. I do not think that it is at all necessary to keep pigs as dirty as they are usually kept," returned Uncle Randolph.

"Say, Uncle," put in Tom, with a sudden twinkle in his eye, "are you going to sell pork by the yard after this?"

"By the yard?" queried Uncle Randolph, and then a faint smile flickered over his face. "Oh, I see! You mean sausage lengths, eh?"

"Not exactly, although that is one way of selling pork by the yard," returned Tom. "I was thinking of what happened in our college town. One of the boys went into a butcher's shop, and asked for a yard of pork, and the butcher handed out three pig's feet."

"Oh, what a rusty joke, Tom!" exclaimed Sam.

"Well, I didn't ask for the yard of pork; it was Dobson who did that," returned Tom, coolly.

Having inspected the various improvements, the boys returned to the house, and then went upstairs for another short talk with their father. In the midst of this, the family physician arrived. When he had waited on the invalid, the boys called the doctor to one side, and asked him to tell them the truth regarding their parent.

"Oh, I think he'll pull through all right," said the doctor. "But as I have told your uncle and your aunt, he must be kept quiet. If you talk business to him, or excite him in any way, it is bound to make matters worse."

"Then we'll keep him just as quiet as possible," returned Tom. "If anything unusual occurs in his business, we won't let him know anything about it."

"That would be best," answered the doctor, gravely; and took his departure.

Several days passed, and by that time the boys felt once more quite at home. Once they went out in the touring car, taking their aunt and uncle along.

"It's too bad we can't take dad," was Sam's comment, "but the doctor says it won't do. We'll have to leave him in charge of Aleck." The ride proved a most enjoyable one, and the older folks were much pleased by it.

"What do you say, Tom, if we go down to the river and have a swim?" proposed Sam, the next morning. It was an unusually hot day, and the thought of getting into the cool water of the old swimming hole appealed strongly to the youth.

"Suits me," returned his brother. "We haven't had a swim down there since last year."

"You young gents want to be careful about that there swimmin' hole," put in Jack Ness, who had heard the talk.

"Why, what's the matter now, Jack?"

"I dunno, exactly, but I hear some of the fellers sayin' as how that swimmin' hole wasn't safe no more. I think it's on account of the tree roots a growin' there."

"We'll be on our guard," answered Sam, and a little later the two lads set off. It was a long walk over the fields and through the patch of woods skirting the stream, and on arriving at the old swimming hole, Sam and Tom were glad enough to rest awhile before venturing into the water. As my old readers know, the stream was a swiftly-flowing one, and the water was rather cool.

"Remember the day we flew over this way in the biplane?" said Tom. "That sure was some adventure!"

"Yes, but it wasn't a patch to the adventure we had when the biplane was wrecked," returned his brother, referring to a happening which has been related in detail in "The Rover Boys in New York."

Having rested awhile, the two boys started to get ready for their swim. Both had just thrown off their coats, when there came a sudden cry from up the river.

"What's that, Tom?" questioned Sam.

"Somebody is calling. Listen!" and then both boys strained their ears for what might follow.

"There! Stay where you are! Don't move!"

"I can't stay here," said another voice.

"Shall I shoot him now?" put in a heavy bass voice.

"No, wait a minute, I am coming over," said still another voice, and then there was silence. The Rover boys looked at each other in amazement. What did the talk mean?

"Say, sounds to me as if somebody was in trouble!" exclaimed Sam.

"Perhaps we had better go and see," returned Tom.

"All right, but we don't want to get into trouble ourselves. Those fellows, whoever they are, or at least one of them, seems to be armed."

"We'll take a few stones along, Sam, and a couple of sticks, too, if we can find them."

Stones were to be had in plenty, and having picked up several of them, and cast their eyes around for a couple of clubs, the lads lost no time in making their way towards the spot from whence the voices had proceeded. This was at a point where the river made a turn and was divided by a long, narrow island into two channels. The island was covered with brushwood, while the banks of the stream were lined with overhanging trees.

"Now, I am going to shoot him!" cried one of the voices which the boys had heard before.

"No, don't do it, just wait a minute!" answered some one else.

"Maybe they have got some poor fellow, and have robbed him," suggested Sam, as he and his brother hurried forward as quickly as the trees and tangled brushwood would permit.

"One thing is certain, that fellow, whoever he is, is in trouble," returned Tom. "Perhaps we had better yell to those other fellows to stop."

"If we do that, they may shoot the poor chap, and then run away."

"That's so, too! Well, come ahead, let's hurry and see if we can catch sight of them." And then the two boys pushed ahead faster than ever.

Presently the youths came to where there were a number of high rocks covered with trailing vines. As, to avoid these, it would have been necessary to wade in the stream, and thus get their shoes and stockings wet, they began to scramble over the rocks with all possible speed.

"Listen! They are talking again!" exclaimed Sam.

"Grab him! Grab him by the throat!"

"That's all right, Jim, but I don't want the boat to upset," growled another voice.

"Say, you fellows make me tired!" roared the heavy bass voice. "Do you want to keep us here all day?"

"What do you know about this gun? Maybe it will explode."

"Say, Sam, I don't know what to make of this!" panted Tom, who was almost out of breath from the violence of his exertion.

"Maybe they are tramps, and are holding somebody up. Anyway, it sounds bad," returned his brother.

Hauling themselves at last to the top of the rocks, the Rover boys looked ahead. Down in the swiftly-flowing stream, they saw a flat-bottom boat containing two men. One man, a tall, burly individual, had a much smaller fellow by the throat, and was bending him backward. Close at hand, on the shore, stood another man, gun in hand, and with the weapon aimed at the burly individual.

"Now then, shoot!" yelled somebody from the shore of the island opposite, and an instant later the gun went off with a bang. As the report died away, the burly man in the boat relaxed his hold on the other fellow, threw up his arms, and fell over into the river with a loud splash.

CHAPTER XV.
A TELEGRAM OF IMPORTANCE

The Rover boys were horrified by what they saw, and for the instant they neither moved nor spoke. They saw the small man in the boat look over the side into the stream where his assailant had plunged from sight, then this fellow caught up a single oar that remained in the craft, and commenced to paddle quickly to shore.

"Oh, Tom, they have killed him!" gasped Sam, on recovering from the shock.

"It certainly looks like it, Sam," returned Tom. "If he wasn't shot dead, he must be drowned. Come on!" and, heedless of possible danger, Tom scrambled down from the rocks and hurried towards the men, with Sam close behind him. They had not yet reached the pair on the river bank, when, to their amazement, they saw the burly individual who had gone overboard, reappear at a point further down the stream. He was swimming lustily for shore.

"Hello! He can't be so badly hurt!" exclaimed Tom. "Look at him strike out!"

"Maybe he was only scared, and went overboard to escape a second shot," suggested Sam.

"Hi! you fellows over there!" yelled the man who carried the gun. "Was that all right?"

"It looked so to me, although you were a little slow about it," came from the shore of the island; and now, glancing in that direction, Sam and Tom saw two men. One had what looked to be a megaphone in his hand, and the second stood behind a high, thin camera with a handle attached, set on a tripod. At the sight of the camera, both youths stopped short. Then Tom looked at his brother and began to snicker.

"Sold! What do you think of that, Sam?"

"Why, they are only taking a moving picture!" exclaimed the younger Rover. "Talk about a sell, Tom! That's one on us."

"Don't let them know how we were sold," returned the brother, quickly. "If it leaked out we'd never hear the end of it."

"Right you are! Mum's the word!" And it may be added here that the boys kept their word, and said nothing to those at home about how they had been fooled.

By the time they reached the man in the boat and the fellow with the gun, the individual who had gone overboard was coming up the river bank, dripping water with every step.

"Say, was that all right?" he demanded, as he stripped off his coat and wrung the water from it. "I hope it was, because I don't want to go through that again, not even for the extra five dollars."

"So you are taking moving pictures," remarked Tom, pleasantly. "That was sure a great scene."

"Oh, so you saw it, did you?" returned the man with a gun. "I thought we were here all alone," and he did not seem to be particularly pleased over the boys' arrival.

"Going to take some more pictures here?" questioned Sam.

"That's our business," answered the man in the boat, crustily.

"Well, maybe it's ours, too," returned the youngest Rover, quickly, not liking the manner in which he had been addressed. "This land belongs to my folks."

"Oh, is that it?" cried the man, and now he looked a bit more pleasant. "Are you the Rovers?"

"Yes."

"No, we are about done with our picture taking in this vicinity," continued the man in the boat. "The next picture in this series is to be at the railroad station at Oak Run."

"Say, I would like to get into some of those movies," remarked Tom. "I imagine it would be a lot of fun."

"Not if you've got to go overboard as I did," grumbled the man who was wet. "Talk about the strenuous life, this takes the cake! Why, in the past ten days, I have gone over a cliff, rescued two women from a burning tenement house, climbed a rope hanging from a burning balloon, and fallen off a moving freight car. Can you beat that for action?"

"Certainly some stunts!" answered Tom. "But one must get a lot of fun out of it."

"Oh, sure! Especially when one of the women you are saving from the burning house gets nervous for fear the flames will reach her, and grabs you by the ear and nearly pulls it off," growled the moving picture actor.

"Say!" yelled the man with the megaphone. "Aren't you coming over here to get us?"

"Of course," returned the man in the boat, hastily. "Bill, give me that other oar," he went on, and having secured the blade, he lost no time in rowing over to the island. In the meanwhile, the fellow with the camera had dismounted the moving picture machine and folded up the tripod, and was ready to depart.

"Would you mind telling me what this picture is going to be called?" asked Sam. "We would like to know so, if we see it advertised anywhere, we can take a look at it."

"This is scene twenty-eight from 'His Last Chance,'" answered the man with the gun.

"All right, we'll take a chance on 'His Last Chance' when we get the chance," answered Tom with a grin, and at this play on words the moving picture men smiled. Soon they had packed all their belongings, and, getting into the boat, they started down the stream for a landing some distance below.

"We're a fine set of heroes," remarked Sam, grinningly, as he and Tom walked back in the direction of the swimming hole. "Wouldn't it have been rich if we had rushed in to save that fellow in the boat, and spoiled the picture."

"Don't mention it, Sam," pleaded Tom. "That sure was one on us." And then both laughed heartily over the way they had been fooled.

Reaching the swimming hole, it did not take the youths long to get into the water. Remembering what Jack Ness had said about being careful, they moved around cautiously.

"Here is a tree root that ought to be removed," remarked Sam, after diving down. "A fellow could easily catch fast on it."

"Maybe we had better put up a danger sign," suggested his brother, and getting out a note book he carried, he tore a page from it and wrote as follows:

DANGER!

Look Out for the Tree Roots!

"There! That ought to do some good," he went on, as he pinned the notice fast to the nearest tree trunk. The boys enjoyed their swim thoroughly. They indulged in many monkey-shines, and also had a little race to the opposite bank and back. This race was won by Tom, but Sam proved a very close second.

"Now then, I guess we had better hurry home, or we may be late for lunch," said Sam, after consulting his watch. "It is quarter of twelve."

Much refreshed, the lads started back for the farmhouse. They were still some distance away when they saw Jack Ness hurrying towards them.

"I say, gents!" called out the hired man. "You're wanted at the house right away."

"What's the matter, Jack?" demanded Tom, quickly. "Is father worse?"

"No, it ain't that, Master Tom. It's a telegram what come for you."

"A telegram?" repeated Sam. "Do you know where it is from?"

"Your uncle said it was from Mr. Dick."

"Then there must be important news," said Tom, and without further words both youths started on a swift gait for the house. Their aunt and uncle saw them coming, and ran out on the back porch to meet them. Their aunt held up her hand warningly.

"Now don't make any noise, boys," she pleaded. "We must not disturb your father."

"What is it? What's the news?"

"It's a telegram from Dick," answered their Uncle Randolph. "I can't quite make it out, but, evidently, it is very important. Here it is."

He fumbled in the pocket of his coat, and brought forth the yellow envelope and handed it to Tom. Taking out the telegram, the youth read it, with Sam looking over his shoulder. It ran as follows:

"If possible, I want Sam and Tom to come to New York at once. Very important. Do not alarm father.

"Richard Rover."

"What do you make of this, Tom?" asked Sam, after he had read the telegram several times.

"I don't know what to make of it, Sam. But one thing is certain: Dick needs us. Something out of the ordinary has happened."

"That is just what I think, boys," put in their uncle. "Maybe I had better go with you," he added, nervously.

"No, no, Randolph. You stay here with me," pleaded his wife. "The boys can attend to the New York matters better than you can." She knew her husband well, and realized that he was decidedly backward when it came to the transaction of business matters of importance. He was wrapped up in his books and his theories about scientific farming and was a dreamer in the largest sense of that word.

"Very well, my dear, just as you say," answered the uncle, meekly.

"Boys, you won't disturb your father, will you?" continued their Aunt Martha, anxiously. "You know the doctor said he must not be disturbed under any circumstances."

"Have you told him about this telegram?" questioned Sam.

"Not a word."

"Then we had better keep still. We can tell him that we want to go to New York just to see Dick and Dora," put in Tom. And so it was arranged.

By consulting a new timetable, the boys found they could make a good railroad connection for the metropolis by taking a train that left Oak Run at three-thirty o'clock. This would give them about three hours in which to get lunch, pack their suitcases, and bid good-bye to their father.

Mr. Rover was somewhat surprised when his sons told him that they were going to New York to see Dick and his newly-made wife, but they smoothed matters over by stating that they found it rather dull on the farm.

"We'd like to go if you can spare us," said Sam.

"Oh, yes, boys, go by all means if you would like to," returned Mr. Rover, quickly. "I can get along very well. Your Aunt Martha is a splendid nurse—and you mustn't forget that I have Aleck."

"An' you can depend upon Aleck, ebery time, sah," put in the colored man, with a broad grin that showed all of his ivories.

"We are going to try to surprise Dick," said Tom. "We are going to take the afternoon train." And then, after a few more words with their father, and without letting him suspect in the least why they were going to New York, the two lads bade him an affectionate farewell and left the room.

"Better take a good supply of clothing along, Sam," remarked Tom, when they were packing up. "There is no telling how long we'll have to remain in the city."

"What do you suppose it is all about, Tom?" questioned the younger brother, anxiously.

"It's about business, that's certain. More than likely Dick has run into more trouble." But how great that trouble was, neither of the boys realized.

CHAPTER XVI.
THE MOVING PICTURE

When the two Rover boys arrived at the railroad station at Oak Run, they were a little surprised to find themselves once more confronted by the moving picture people they had met on the river.

"Hello! So you are following us up, are you?" said the man who had handled the gun. But he smiled as he spoke, because he saw that the boys carried dresssuit cases and were equipped for traveling.

"Have you taken your picture of the railroad station yet?" questioned Tom.

"We've had one scene in front of the ticket office," returned the man. "But our main scene we shall pull off when the train comes in— or rather, when it pulls out."

"Perhaps you'll want us in it, after all," broke in Sam.

"See here! If you fellows want to get in this picture, just say so and I guess I can arrange it," said the man who had handled the megaphone in the scene on the river, and who was, evidently, the director of the company.

"That depends on what you want us to do," declared Tom.

"Oh, you won't have much to do. You see, it's like this," went on the manager. "This man who did the shooting wants to escape. He runs up to the railroad station here and buys his ticket—we have that part of it already. Then he is supposed to be in hiding behind yonder freighthouse. When the train comes in, he waits for all other passengers to get on board, then, as the train pulls out, he rushes forward and catches on the last car. At the same time one of the other fellows rushes out as if to catch him, but he is too late. Now, if you want to get into the scene, you get on the train just before she starts and stand on the back platform."

"Let's do it, Tom; it will be quite a lark!" exclaimed Sam.

"I'm willing," answered his brother; and so the matter was arranged. Then the boys hurried into the ticket office, to get their tickets to New York.

In the office they found old man Ricks, the station agent, grumbling to himself.

"Wot ye want?" he demanded, sourly, as he looked at the Rovers.

"Two tickets to New York, Mr. Ricks," returned Tom. "What's the matter?"

"Wot's the matter, huh? A whole lot, I should say!" declared old Ricks, as he began to make out the tickets. "A lot o' them movin' picter fellers been in here cuttin' up like mad."

"What did they do?" asked Sam, curiously.

"Huh! what didn't they do?" retorted the station master. "Come in here, an' knocked over a box an' a basket, rushed up to the winder, an' the next thing I knew, he had planked down a lot o' money, an' when I stuck my head out the winder here, that feller pretended to grab up a ticket wot I didn't give him at all, an' took up his money and dusted out the door. At the same time while this was goin' on, 'nother feller had a light turned on this here winder wot nearly blinded me, and the feller with that funny lookin' camera was a-turnin' the crank to beat the cars!"

"They were only taking a moving picture, Mr. Ricks," declared Sam. "You shouldn't object to that."

"Huh! I ain't hired by the railroad company to get in no movin' picter," growled the station master. "I'm here to 'tend to the railroad business, and nothin' else."

"Never mind, Mr. Ricks, if they've got you in the picture you ought to be proud of it," declared Tom. "Think of the millions and millions of people all over the world who will be looking at you when they visit the moving picture theaters."

"Huh! I ain't no movin' picter actor, I ain't," snorted old Ricks. "I'm a decent, respectable member o' this community, an' I'm a church member, too. I ain't got no use for them movin' picter shows. It's a waste o' good money, that's jest wot it is," and then Ricks shuffled off to attend to some baggage that had come in.

With their tickets in their pockets, the two Rover boys rejoined the moving picture company on the railroad platform. They were quite interested in watching the camera man set up his machine, and asked him several questions regarding its operation. Then they heard a well-known whistle down the track, and knew that their train was coming.

"All ready, there!" cried the manager of the moving picture company. "Now, don't make a fizzle of it, Jake."

"I won't, unless the train pulls out too quickly," returned Jake. "I am not going to get killed, though."

"Well, you've got to take some chances in this business," said the manager, coolly.

There were six or eight passengers getting off the train, and about an equal number to board the cars. As they had been instructed, the Rover boys got on the rear platform of the last car, and stood in the doorway looking back on the tracks. Tom pretended that he was waving his hand to somebody in the distance.

As the train began to move, and while the camera man was taking the picture, one of the actors, as agreed, rushed across the platform and got hold of the rail of the last step. Then, as he pretended to have hard work to pull himself up, the second actor came running down the platform, shaking his fist at the man who was escaping. Then the train passed out of sight around the bend, and the little moving picture scene came to an end.

"Well, I'm glad that's over," declared he actor, as he followed the boys into the car. "I never like the scenes where I am in danger of getting hurt."

"You certainly must have a strenuous time of it," declared Sam; and then he added quickly: "Are you going to New York with us?"

"Oh, no. I'm to get off at the first station and take another train back to Oak Run. The crowd will wait for me. We have some scenes to do at a farmhouse." And then, as he had a ride of ten minutes, the moving picture man told the boys of some things which had happened to him during his career as a movies' actor.

"How soon do you think they will show that picture?" asked Sam, when the man prepared to leave the train.

"In a week or two," was the answer. "I don't know the exact date for the release;" and then the man said good-bye and left them.

"Do you know, if I didn't have anything else to do, I wouldn't mind going into the moving picture business," remarked Tom, as the train rushed onward. "It must be lots of fun to be in the different scenes."

"Perhaps so, Tom. At the same time, those fellows must put up with a great number of inconveniences. Think of plunging into the water when it is cold, or into a burning building when the thermometer is over a hundred in the shade."

"Oh, I know that, and, come to think of it, I was reading only yesterday about a movies' actor who, in a war scene taken out on the Hackensack meadows, fell into a trench, and broke an arm and also a leg. Just the same, I wouldn't mind trying it."

"Maybe you'll get a chance some day."

On and on went the train, and, with little else to do, the boys discussed the situations at home and in the city.

"One thing is sure, Tom," said the youngest Rover, earnestly. "No matter what happens in New York, we mustn't let father know about it. I think the worry is worse for him than anything else."

"Oh, I agree on that. Even if we lose a lot of money, he must not know one word about it."

"Do you think we'll lose any money?"

"I don't know what to think. One thing is sure, something very much out of the way has happened, or Dick wouldn't have sent that telegram."

"Perhaps Pelter, Japson & Company haven't been as honest as they promised to be. Maybe they are holding back some of the securities that belong to dad."

"That may be so, too. At the same time, you must remember that Songbird's uncle is our attorney, and I don't think Mr. Powell would let them get away with very much. You'll remember what Dick wrote some time ago, that he had taken the office fixtures for part of the debt. That would seem to indicate that he had gotten everything from the firm that he could lay his hands on."

"I wonder if we'll ever meet that Barton Pelter again."

"Perhaps, although if he is a nephew of Jesse Pelter, it is more than likely he will keep out of sight, thinking that a meeting between us would be very unpleasant."

At one of the stops a dining car was attached to the train, and, as the boys were hungry, they lost no time in going in for the evening meal.

"Say, Tom, look there," whispered Sam, during the course of the repast, and, with a look from his eye, he indicated a man sitting on the other side of the car. The fellow was a tall, surly individual, plainly dressed. His face was somewhat flushed, as if he had been drinking.

"Why, that's the head gardener at Hope!" said Tom. "It is queer that he should be on this train, Sam!"

"If you'll remember, he lost his job at the seminary."

"He did? I didn't hear anything of that."

"Oh, yes, Grace told me about it. He was a splendid gardener, but every once in a while he would drink too much, and then get into a quarrel with the other help, so they had to let him go."

"It's a shame that such fellows can't leave drink alone," was Tom's comment.

The man had settled himself, and ordered quite an elaborate dinner. He was in the midst of eating, with the Rover boys paying little attention to him, when he happened to glance at them. He straightened up and stared in astonishment, and then looked decidedly uncomfortable.

"He's looking at us, Tom," whispered Sam.

"Well, let him look if he wants to. It doesn't cost anything," was the reply. And then Tom turned his head squarely, and stared at the former seminary gardener. Immediately, the man dropped his eyes, and went on with his meal. He soon finished, and, paying his bill, left the dining car in a hurry.

"That's a queer way to do," was Sam's comment. "He acted as if he didn't want us to see him."

"Maybe he is ashamed of himself for having lost his position," returned the brother. "Anyway, it's none of our business." And there the talk came to an end.

CHAPTER XVII.
WHAT DICK HAD TO TELL

"Here we are, Sam!"

"And I'm glad of it, Tom. I don't care much about riding in the cars after it is too dark to look out of the windows," returned the youngest Rover.

The train was nearing the Grand Central Terminal, in New York City. The passengers were gathering their belongings, and the porter was moving from one to another, brushing them and gathering in his tips. Then the train rushed into the long station, and soon came to a halt.

"I wonder if Dick will be on hand to meet us?" said Sam, as he and his brother left the car and made their way towards the waiting-room.

"Maybe, although it's pretty late."

There was a large crowd coming and going, and, for the moment, the lads had all they could do to get through. Then, as they emerged into the middle of the big waiting-room, they saw two familiar figures close at hand.

"Hello, Dick! How do you do, Dora!"

"So here you are, Tom and Sam!" cried their big brother, and shook hands heartily. Then Dora came up to greet the newcomers.

"Did you have a nice trip?" asked Dick's wife, as she smiled at them.

"Oh, yes, it was all right," answered Sam. "And what do you think? We got in a moving picture!"

"You did!" exclaimed Dora. "That certainly is a new experience."

"We received your telegram, Dick," said Tom, and looked at his big brother, anxiously. "I hope nothing very serious has happened."

"Well, Tom, I—I——" Twice Dick tried to go on and failed. He looked at both of his brothers, and his face showed something that they had never seen in it before.

"Oh, Dick! Don't say anything here!" interposed Dora, hastily. "Wait till we get to the hotel." She turned to Sam and Tom. "Don't ask him any questions now. It won't do to have a scene here."

"All right, Dora, just as you say," answered Tom, quickly. Yet, both he and Sam wondered greatly what had occurred to so upset Dick.

The oldest Rover boy had a taxicab handy, and into this the whole party got and were quickly driven across Forty-second Street to Fifth Avenue, and then, for a number of blocks, down that well-known thoroughfare. Soon they turned towards Broadway, and a moment later came to a stop before the main entrance of the Outlook Hotel.

"As you know, we have a suite of rooms here," said Dick to his brothers. "I have hired an extra room next door, so we can all be together."

A bellboy had already secured the newcomers' baggage, and, after signing the register, Sam and Tom followed Dick and his wife to the elevator and to the third floor.

"It's a fine layout, all right," declared Sam, when they were settled and the bellboy had been dismissed.

Dick did not make any answer to this remark. He walked over to the door, to see that it was closed, then he suddenly wheeled to confront his brothers.

"You've got to know it sooner or later, so you might as well know it now," he said in as steady a voice as he could command. "Do you remember that I wrote to you about sixty-four thousand dollars' worth of bonds that I had bought for dad in place of some securities that he possessed?"

"Yes," answered both brothers.

"Well, those bonds have been stolen."

"Stolen!" gasped Sam.

"You don't mean it, Dick!" came from Tom.

"I do mean it. The bonds have been stolen, and, try my best, I can't get a single clew as to where they went or who took them."

"Sixty-four thousand dollars! Phew!" ejaculated Sam. "That's some loss!"

"But please don't blame Dick," broke in Dora. "I am sure it isn't his fault."

"How did it happen?" questioned Tom.

"They were taken out of the safe at the offices."

"Stolen from the safe, you mean?"

"Yes."

"When was this?"

"Day before yesterday."

"Of course the safe was locked?" put in Sam.

"Certainly."

"But Pelter and Japson knew that combination, didn't they, Dick?" questioned Tom, eagerly.

"No, Tom, they did not. When they turned the offices over to me, Pelter made some sarcastic remark, stating I had better have the combination changed. I told him I certainly would have it changed; and the very next day I had the safe makers up to inspect the lock, and change the combination."

"Humph! Then that lets Pelter and Japson out, doesn't it?"

"But somebody must have taken those bonds," came from Sam. "Did anybody else have the combination, Dick?"

"Nobody but Dora. I gave her the figures, so she could get the safe open in case anything happened to me, or I was away."

"I've got the figures on a card in my pocket-book," explained Dora, "but I don't believe anybody saw them. In fact, the card has nothing but the bare figures on it, so it isn't likely that any one would understand what those figures meant. Oh, but isn't it perfectly dreadful! I—I hope you—you boys won't blame Dick," she faltered.

"Of course we don't blame Dick," returned Tom, promptly.

"Why should we blame him?" added Sam. "If he put the bonds in the safe and locked them up, I can't see how this robbery is his fault. It might have happened to any of us."

"I'm glad to hear you say that," returned Dick; and his face showed his relief. "Just the same, boys, we have got to find those bonds. Our family can't afford to lose sixty-four thousand dollars—or rather sixty thousand dollars."

"What do you mean, Dick?" asked Tom. "You said sixty-four thousand dollars."

"So I did, but four thousand of the bonds were registered in dad's name, principal and interest, so it's likely the thief won't be able to use them."

"And all the other bonds were unregistered?" queried Sam.

"Yes, every one of them."

"So they can be used by any one?"

"Exactly—although, of course, the thief would have to be very careful how he disposed of them."

"Have you notified the police?" asked Tom.

"Not yet. I wanted to consult you first. Besides, I thought it might be possible that the thief would put an advertisement in the newspapers, offering to return the bonds for a reward. But so far, I haven't seen any such advertisement."

"It isn't likely they'll offer to return them if sixty thousand dollars' worth are negotiable," returned Tom. "But give us the particulars of the affair;" and the youth dropped into a seat, and the others did the same.

"Well, to start with, as I said before, as soon as Pelter and Japson and their hired help left, I had the lock of the safe investigated, and then had the combination changed," began Dick. "The fellow from the safe company showed me how the combination was worked, so I fixed the new numbers to suit myself, in order that no outsider would know how to open the safe. I put the numbers down on two cards, and placed one of the cards in my notebook, and gave the other to Dora. As she said, the cards had nothing on them but the bare numbers, so that a person getting one of the cards would not know that the numbers referred to the safe combination.

"It took me several days to get rid of the old stocks, and while I was doing that I, from time to time, purchased the bonds, buying them, on the advice of Mr. Powell, from several bond houses in Wall Street. I also bought a brand new japanned box with a little lock, and placed the bonds in that box, and then put the box in the safe. The last

I saw of the bonds was about half-past four in the afternoon, when I placed the last of the bonds in the box. I came down to the office at a little before ten o'clock the next morning, and opened the safe about half an hour later. Then the box was gone."

"Wait a minute, Dick," interrupted Tom. "You just said you opened the safe. Wasn't the door already open?"

"No, the door was shut and locked, just as I had left it the night before."

"Humph! Then somebody must have worked the combination," ventured Sam.

"So it would seem, Sam, and yet when I had the lock inspected, the safe company man told me that that was a first-class combination, and practically burglar proof."

"Is it an old safe?"

"I don't think so—in fact, the safe man led me to believe it was one of the newer kinds. It is about five feet square, and the walls are almost a foot thick. Oh, it is some safe, I can tell you that!"

"But it was not safe in this instance," retorted Tom, who, no matter how serious the situation, was bound to have his little joke.

"You said Pelter and Japson had gone for good," continued Sam. "Is there nobody else around attached to the old firm?"

"I took on their old office boy, a lad named Bob Marsh. You'll remember him," returned the oldest Rover. "He said he wanted work the worst way, so I thought I would give him a chance."

"Maybe he got the combination, and gave it to Pelter or Japson."

"I don't think so, Sam. The boy is rather forward in his manner, but I think he is perfectly honest."

"Yes, but somebody opened that safe and took the box of bonds," put in Tom.

"I know that, Tom, and we've got to get those bonds back, or it will be a very serious piece of business for us," answered the oldest Rover boy, soberly.

"Was anything else taken, Dick?" questioned Sam.

"Not a thing. And that's queer, too, because I had a number of private papers in the safe, and also our new set of books."

"Then that would go to show that all the thief was after were the bonds," came from Tom. "You say they were in a new japanned box that was locked?"

"Yes, but the lock didn't amount to much. I think it could easily be opened."

"Sixty thousand dollars is a lot of money to lose," mused Sam. "Dick, that will put us in something of a hole, won't it?"

"It may. But don't let us think about that, Sam. Let us try to get the bonds back," returned his oldest brother, earnestly.

CHAPTER XVIII.
AT THE OFFICES

After that the three Rovers and Dick's wife talked the matter over for fully an hour. Dick gave Sam and Tom all the particulars he could think of, and answered innumerable questions. But try their best, not one of the party could venture a solution of the mystery.

"I think you had better go to bed," said Dora, at last. "You can go down to the offices the first thing in the morning, and make up your minds what to do next;" and this advice was followed.

"No use of talking, this is a fierce loss!" was Tom's comment, when he and Sam were retiring.

"Yes, and Dick feels pretty bad over it," returned the youngest Rover. "I am afraid he imagines that we think he is to blame."

"Maybe, but I don't blame him, Sam. That might have happened to you or me just as well as to him."

It must be admitted that the boys did not sleep very soundly that night. For a long time each lay awake, speculating over the mystery, and wondering what had become of the bonds.

"Perhaps Pelter and Japson had nothing at all to do with it," thought Tom, as he reviewed the situation. "It may have been some outsider, who watched Dick alter the combination of the safe."

All of the boys were up early in the morning, and accompanied by Dora, obtained breakfast in the hotel dining-room.

"If you want me to go along, I shall be glad to do so," said Dora, during the course of the meal. It cut her to the heart to have Dick so troubled.

"No, Dora, you had better stay here, or else spend your time shopping," answered Dick. "We'll have to take care of this matter ourselves."

"I'll tell you what you can do," broke in Tom. "You can write a nice letter to Aunt Martha, telling her that we have arrived safely, and that we are going into some business matters with Dick. Of course, you needn't say a word about the robbery. It will be time enough to tell her and Uncle Randolph after we have tried all we can to get the bonds back—and failed."

As my old readers will probably remember, the offices formerly occupied by Pelter, Japson & Company were located at the lower end of Wall Street. The building was an old one, five stories in height, which had recently been put in repair. The offices were on the fourth floor in the extreme rear, and had a fairly good outlook.

The Rovers found the office boy, Bob Marsh, already on hand, and doing some work which Dick had given him. He was a bright, sharp-eyed lad, his only failing being that he was a bit forward.

"Any one here to see me, Bob?" asked Dick, as they entered.

"Nobody, sir, but an agent that wanted to sell you some kind of a new calendar. I told him we had bushels of calendars already," and the boy grinned slightly.

Passing through two small offices, the Rovers came to one in the rear—that which had formerly been used by Jesse Pelter.

"Looks a little bit familiar," observed Tom. "Looks like when I visited it as Roy A. Putnam, from Denver, Colorado, and thought about taking stock in the Irrigation Company," and he laughed shortly as he recalled that incident, the particulars of which have been related in "The Rover Boys in New York."

"You've got pretty big offices for only you and the office boy," remarked Sam.

"I took them just as the old concern had them," returned Dick. "But if business increases, I guess we'll have to have quite some office help. Anyway, a bookkeeper and a stenographer."

"Hadn't you better send that office boy out for a little while?" suggested Sam.

"A good idea," returned his oldest brother, and sent the lad on an errand up to the post-office.

Left to themselves, the Rovers once more went over the details of the robbery so far as they knew them. Dick opened the safe, showing his brothers how the combination lock was worked; then the boys looked inside the strong-box, and into the private compartment which, so Dick told them, had contained the missing box of bonds.

"I don't see how they got into this safe," was Sam's comment, after the door had been closed and the combination turned on. "I can't make head or tail of how to get it open."

"Let me have a try at it," returned Tom, and he worked for several minutes over the combination.

"Here are the figures for the combination," said Dick, and he turned them over to his brothers. But even with the figures before them, they found it no easy task to open the heavy door of the strong-box. This door was provided with several bolts, so that to get it open without either working the combination or else blowing the door open, was out of the question.

"It's a Chinese puzzle to me. I give it up," declared Tom, at last. "The only way I imagine, Dick, is that, somehow or other, somebody got hold of that combination."

"It would seem so, Tom. But I can't see how it could be done, or who did it," was the answer.

"Do you suppose that boy suspects anything?" questioned Sam.

"He may, because, after I discovered that the box was gone, I questioned him pretty closely as to who had been in the offices. I guess he knows something is wrong."

"Let us ask him about Pelter and Japson when he comes back," said Tom. "It certainly won't do any harm to get all the information possible. Then, if we can't get any clew by noon, I think the best thing you can do, Dick, is to notify the authorities."

It was not long before Bob Marsh came back from his errand to the post-office, and then Dick called him into the inner office.

"Now, Bob, I'm going to tell you something," said the oldest Rover, coming to the point without delay. "There has been a robbery here."

"Robbery!" exclaimed the boy. "I didn't do it. I wouldn't take nothin'," he went on, quickly.

"I didn't say you did, Bob. But what I want you to do is to tell me everything that you know. Was there anybody in this office during my absence?"

"Nobody went into this office while I was here," declared the office boy. "I wouldn't let 'em in. But then you must remember, the janitors come in during the night to clean up."

"Oh, yes, I know that."

"Dick, do you think the janitor of the building could be in this?" exclaimed Sam.

"As I have said several times, I don't know what to think," answered Dick. "As a matter of fact, I don't know who the janitor is."

"Say!" broke in the office boy, suddenly. "There was one feller here that I didn't tell you about. I forgot about him. He was here three or four days ago—I don't exactly remember what day it was."

"Who was that?"

"Why, it was a young feller named Barton Pelter. He's a relation to Mr. Pelter. I think Mr. Pelter is his uncle."

"Barton Pelter!" exclaimed Dick. He looked at his brothers. "That must be the same fellow that you wrote about—the fellow you pulled out of the river."

"What did this Barton Pelter want?" asked Sam.

"He wanted to see his uncle. He knew that the firm had sold out to you folks, but he was not certain if they had moved away yet. When I told him that his uncle was gone, he looked kind of disappointed."

"Was he in this office, Bob?" questioned Dick.

"No, sir, he was only in the outside office."

"Did he say anything about bonds or money?"

"No, sir."

"Say, tell me something!" broke in Tom. "Were this Barton Pelter and his uncle on good terms?"

"They used to be," replied the office boy, "but once or twice they had some pretty warm talks. This young feller didn't like it at all the way his uncle treated your father. I heard him tell his uncle once, that what he was doing was close to swindling. Then Mr. Pelter got awful mad, and told him he had better get out."

"Good for Barton!" murmured Sam. "He can't be such a bad sort."

"Oh, I guess he was all right," put in the office boy, with the freedom that seemed natural to him. "Only I guess he was dependent on his uncle for money. Maybe if it wasn't for that, he would have pitched into his uncle more than he did. But say! You said something was stolen. What was it?"

"Sixty-four thousand dollars in bonds," answered Dick.

"What! Say, boss, ain't you kiddin'?" and the boy looked incredulous.

"No, it is the truth, Bob. Somebody took a box out of that safe that contained sixty-four thousand dollars' worth of bonds."

"Great smoke! I didn't think there was that many bonds in the hull building!" cried the boy, with emphasis.

"I only expected to keep them here a few days," went on Dick. "Later on, of course, I would have placed them in a safe deposit vault."

"Say, boss! you sure don't think that I took them bonds?" cried the office boy.

"No, I don't, Bob. But somebody took them, and we've got to find them."

"Sure, we've got to find them!" cried Bob. "Say, do you want me to call the janitor? Maybe he knows something about it."

"Yes, you may call him, but don't tell him what we want him for," answered Dick.

CHAPTER XIX.
THE FIRST CLEW

The janitor of the building was Mike Donovan, an aged Irishman, who was assisted in his work by his wife and his daughter Kittie, aged about fifteen.

"'Tis me yez want to see?" queried Donovan, as he shuffled into the inner office, hat in hand.

"You are the janitor of this building?" questioned Dick, looking him over carefully.

"I am that, sur."

"Can you tell me who is in the habit of cleaning this particular office?"

"Well, sur, we are all after takin' a hand at it. I ginerally do the swapin', and me wife or Kittie, me daughter, do the winder clanin' an' the dustin'."

"During the past four or five days, have you noticed anything unusual around this office?" went on Dick.

"Phat are ye after mainin'?"

"I'll tell you. There has been a robbery here, and we want to get at the bottom of it."

"I haven't touched a thing, sur, an' nather have me family!" cried the janitor, quickly.

"You look like an honest man, and I can't say that I suspect you," continued Dick, for he saw that the old janitor was evidently much hurt. "I want you to help me all you can, that is all."

"Sure, sur, an' I'll be after doin' that, Mr. Rover. Phat did they be after takin'?"

"This safe, here, has been looted, and a small box that contained sixty-four thousand dollars' worth of bonds is gone."

At this announcement the old janitor threw up both hands and faltered back a step or two.

"Sixty-four thousand, dollars, did you be after sayin'?" he gasped, thinking he had not heard aright.

"That is what I said. Now then, just put on your thinking cap, and see if you can remember anything unusual that happened around here two or three days ago."

"Two or three days ago. Let me see," mused the janitor, scratching his head. "I don't remember anything—Oh, yes, I do!" he burst out.

"What was that?" queried all three of the Rovers, while the office boy looked on with mouth wide open.

"'Twas one avenin' about siven or eight o'clock. Me an' me family were up stairs, clanin' out an office that has just been rinted. Kittie, me gurrel, wint down stairs for some extra dustin' rags. Whin she came back, she said she saw a man a-walkin' through the hallway outside. She said that as soon as he saw her, he didn't wait for the illevator, but went down the stairs in a big hurry."

"Did she know the man?"

"She did not. At least, she said she didn't recognize him, for, you see, there was only one little light burnin' in the hallway, because nearly all the tinnents had gone home. The illevator wouldn't have been runnin', only we was goin' to take up the stuff to the office we was cleanin' on the fifth floor."

"Your daughter saw that man in the hallway?" questioned Tom. "Did he seem to come from these offices?"

"No, I axed her particular, and she said he seemed to be comin' from the back av the hall."

"What is back there?" asked Sam.

"A winder wid a fire escape outside," answered the janitor. "Likewise, I've a sink closet there, where I keep me brooms and me brushes and such."

"And you have no idea who the man was?" questioned Dick.

"No, sur. I axed Kitty how he looked, but she said she hadn't seen his face—that he turned away from her and went down the stairs as fast as he could."

"More than likely that was the thief!" exclaimed Tom. "The question is: Who is he and where did he go?"

"Did your daughter say how the man was dressed?" asked Sam.

"Sure! She said he had on a dark suit of clothes and a dark, soft hat. That's all she knew."

"Was he a big man?"

"Oh, she said he was about middlin' big."

This was all the old janitor could tell, and a little later he brought in both his wife and his daughter to be interviewed. The girl was almost scared to death, and could add nothing to what her father had already told.

"Well, it's a clew, even if it is a slight one," was Tom's comment. "Dick, I guess the best thing you can do is to call up police headquarters."

"I'll do it. But please remember one thing," went on the oldest Rover boy, turning to the janitor and his family and also the office boy. "We want to keep this as quiet as possible for the present, so please don't say anything about it." And all of them promised to keep silent.

It did not take long for Dick to get into communication with the authorities, and after a short talk over the telephone, he was told that a couple of detectives would be sent down to his once without delay.

"Have you told Mr. Powell?" questioned Tom, suddenly.

"No, but I will call him up now," answered his older brother.

Of course the lawyer was astonished at the news, and asked what steps had been taken to apprehend the thief. When told that the authorities had been asked to take charge of the case, he wanted to know if he could be of any assistance.

"I don't see how you can help us, Mr. Powell," answered Dick, over the wire. "I suppose we will have to put the whole matter in the hands of the police."

"Well, if I can do anything at all, let me know," answered Songbird's uncle. "I am rather busy now, but as soon as I am at leisure, I will call and talk the matter over with you."

Inside of half an hour the two detectives from headquarters arrived. They were bright, sharp-eyed individuals, and they got down to business without delay. They asked Dick innumerable questions, and looked carefully at the safe, trying the combination several times, and then inspected the offices and the hallway. After that they subjected Kittie Donovan to a close examination, getting the girl to tell everything she could possibly think of regarding the strange man she had seen on the evening when the robbery had occurred.

"I think I know who did this job," said one of the detectives to the other.

"Looks like the work of one of three men to me," returned the other sleuth. "Baldy Jackson, Slim Martin, or Hank the Bluffer."

"You may be right, Joe, but I think it was Hank. If I've got the dope right, those other two fellows you mention are not near New York just now."

"Well, if Baldy and Slim can prove that they weren't around New York at the time, then I'll agree with you that it was Hank who lifted that box," returned the other detective.

"Who is this Hank the Bluffer?" questioned Dick, curiously.

"Oh, he's an old one at this sort of game," returned one of the detectives. "He is a wonder at opening safes. Somebody told me once that he made the assertion he could open any ordinary office safe inside of fifteen minutes. He's got it all in his finger ends. They are so sensitive that when he turns the safe knob, he can feel every movement of the tumblers inside."

"And he is at liberty now?" asked Sam.

"He was the last I heard of him. He got out of a Massachusetts prison about three months ago. Somebody told me he was in New York. I haven't seen him, but if he is here I think we can round him up sooner or later."

"Well, what we want are those bonds," declared Dick.

"Oh, sure! That's what we'll go after," declared the detective. "Even if we locate our man, we won't arrest him until we can get him with the goods."

Following this conversation, the detectives made a memorandum of all the bonds that had been taken, along with the numbers thereon.

"If the thief is an old one at the game, it's not likely that he'll try to use those registered bonds," said one of the detectives, "but he'll find plenty of places where he can use the others, if he knows the game."

"I'm inclined to agree with you on one point," said Dick. "And that is that no ordinary person could have worked the combination of that safe. It must have been some professional."

"You are right, Mr. Rover—unless somebody got the figures of the combination on the sly," answered the sleuth; and a few minutes later he and his fellow-officer left, promising to make a report as soon as anything worth while was brought to light.

Having gotten rid of the detectives and also of the janitor and his family, the Rover boys shut themselves in the inner office to discuss the situation. They had requested the authorities to keep the whole matter quiet for the present, and this the detectives had agreed to do.

"Now, first of all, Dick, tell us: Will this loss affect any of our other investments?" asked Tom.

"Not for the present, Tom, but how we shall stand later on if the securities are not recovered, I am not prepared to say." Dick's face clouded. "You see, it is this way: We have our investments in the West as well as those we went into in Boston some time ago. We—that is, dad—was going to take a loan on that mining proposition. That would involve our putting up some of those bonds—say forty or fifty thousand dollars' worth—as collateral security with the banks. Now, if we don't get the bonds back, dad will either have to cancel that loan or, otherwise, put up something else as security—and what else we can put up just now, I don't know. It's a bad state of affairs."

"Oh, we've just got to get those bonds back!" cried Sam, impulsively. "We've just got to!"

"Easy enough to say, Sam, but wishing them back isn't going to bring them back," came from Tom, grimly.

"If we only had a little more of a clew to work on, we, ourselves, might try to get those bonds back instead of relying on the detectives," said Dick. "But when you haven't any clews, how are you going to strike out?"

"We might try to find that strange man, whoever he is," suggested Tom. "Although looking for him would be a good deal like looking for the proverbial pin in the haystack. I would rather dig up the whole of the Atlantic seacoast looking for Captain Kidd's treasure;" and he smiled grimly.

CHAPTER XX.
BARTON PELTER AGAIN

"Well, Dick, any news?"

"No, Tom. It's the same old story."

"Haven't the detectives been able to locate that fellow they thought might be guilty?" put in Sam.

"No, Sam. They told me up at headquarters that all of the three former criminals one of the detectives mentioned, were nowhere near New York, so far as they could learn."

"Then if they haven't been near this city, that supposition of theirs falls through," was Tom's comment. "What do they propose to do next?"

"I don't think they know. Anyway, they didn't give me any satisfaction;" and, hanging up his hat, Dick sank into an office chair, looking much downcast.

Several days had passed, and during that time the Rover boys had done their best to get further clews concerning the robbery. From an old man who kept an apple stand near the entrance of the building, they had learned that the strange fellow who had been seen by Kittie Donovan was a man of perhaps forty years of age, with a clean-shaven face. But more than that the street merchant was unable to say.

"And there are thousands of men in New York City who are about that age and who have clean-shaven faces," had been Sam's comment on learning this. "That clew won't get us anywhere. Now, if the fellow had limped, or had a crooked nose——"

"Sure! And a false tooth with two spots of gold and a diamond in it, and all that sort of thing," Tom had broken in. "Say, Sam, what do you want, some clews made to order?" and he had laughed grimly.

"I must confess, I am at my wits' end," said Dick.

"What did Mr. Powell have to say about it?" questioned Tom, for he and Sam had been out hunting for clews when the lawyer had called.

"What could he say? He wasn't here when the bonds were taken. He asked me about our other investments; and he said if we got into any financial difficulties through this loss, he would aid us all he could."

"Bully for Songbird's uncle!" cried Sam. "He's as generous as Songbird himself."

"What's bothering me is this," continued the oldest Rover boy. "Sooner or later, if we don't recover those bonds, we have got to let dad know about the loss; and how he is going to take it, I don't know."

"Oh, let us keep it from him just as long as possible," broke in Sam, entreatingly. "Why, Dick, you haven't any idea how run down he is, and how nervous!"

"Oh, yes, I have, Sam. And that is what is worrying me. I don't know if we are doing right to keep this from him."

"Before we tell him anything, let us consult Uncle Randolph and Aunt Martha," said Tom. "If they know the truth, that will lift a little of the responsibility from our shoulders."

"I am not going to tell any of them—at least, not for a week or so longer," returned Dick. "I am living in hope every day that we'll get some kind of a clew."

It had rained hard the day previous, but now the sky was clear. With but little to do in the offices that afternoon after three o'clock, the Rover boys took a walk up Broadway from Wall Street to where the Outlook Hotel was located.

"It certainly is a busy city," was Tom's comment, as they came to a temporary halt in front of the post-office. "Just look at the stream of humanity and the cars and wagons, not to speak of the automobiles."

"What takes my eye, is the size of so many of these buildings," declared Sam. "Say, maybe an earthquake around here wouldn't do some damage!"

"And to think of the way the people travel!" broke in Dick. "They are down in the ground, on the street, and up in the air," and he smiled a little at the thought.

Walking past the post-office, the three youths entered City Hall Park, crossing the same to look at some of the bulletin boards put out by the newspapers located on Park Row.

"Hello!" cried Tom, suddenly; and caught each of his brothers by the arm.

"What now, Tom?" asked Dick, quickly.

"See that fellow over there, leaning against the fence, reading a newspaper?"

"Why, I declare! It is Barton Pelter!" ejaculated Sam.

"You mean Jesse Pelter's nephew—the chap you hauled out of the river?" questioned Dick.

"The same," returned Tom. "Say, I think I'll go over and talk to him," he added, quickly.

"He may not want to talk to you, Tom," interposed his younger brother.

"I'll risk it;" and so speaking, Tom stepped forward and advanced to where the other youth was busy looking over the sporting edition of one of the afternoon sheets.

"What is it? I don't seem to remember you," said Barton Pelter, when Tom touched his arm.

"I am Tom Rover," was the reply. "This is my brother Sam, and this my brother Dick;" and Tom pointed to the others, who were coming up.

"Oh, is that so!" returned Barton Pelter, and put out his hand. "I am glad to see you," he continued, somewhat hesitatingly. "Is this the one who helped to pull me out of the river?" and he nodded towards Sam.

"Yes."

"I am certainly very much obliged to both of you," continued the young man, and his face showed that he meant what he said. "If it hadn't been for you, I might have been drowned. I suppose you—er—you—er—got my letter?"

"Oh, yes, and we understood it, perfectly," returned Tom, hastily. "It's all right. We didn't do so much, after all."

"I think you did a good deal," and Barton Pelter laughed nervously. "You—you are now in business where my uncle used to be, are you not?"

"We are," answered Dick. "By the way, what has become of your uncle?" he questioned, curiously.

"I don't know, exactly. I think though he is going East. Perhaps to Boston. How is business with you?" the young man continued, hastily, as if he wanted to change the subject.

"Oh, business is all right enough," answered Dick. And then he looked meaningly at his brothers.

"The trouble with us is, we've been very unfortunate," broke in Tom, before the others could stop him. "We've just suffered a tremendous loss."

"Is that so? In what way?"

Before answering, Tom looked at Dick. "Shall I tell him?" he questioned, in a low tone.

"You might as well, since you have gone so far," was the reply. "In fact, I don't know that it will do much good to keep still any longer."

"We've been robbed."

"You don't say so! Did you lose much?"

"We lost sixty-four thousand dollars' worth of bonds," answered Sam.

"Oh, a bad business deal, I presume." And Barton Pelter smiled grimly. "That's the way it is in Wall Street. You are up one day, and down the next. That's the way it was with my uncle."

"No, we didn't lose the bonds that way," answered Dick. "They were stolen."

"Stolen! From where?"

"From our office."

"Why, that's the worst I ever heard!" declared Barton Pelter, with interest. "Who was it? Did some fellow sneak into your offices and take them?"

"We don't know how the robbery took place," answered Tom. "My brother put the bonds in a japanned box that was locked, and put the box in the once safe one afternoon. The next morning when he opened the safe, the box with the bonds was gone."

"What's that!" exclaimed the listener, excitedly. "You had them in a box, and put the box in your safe? Do you mean the safe that was in the offices when my uncle and Mr. Japson had it?"

"Sure! it's the same safe," answered Dick.

"Well, what do you know about that!" gasped Barton Pelter. His face showed increasing interest. "When was all this?"

"Just about a week ago."

"Haven't you any clews to the robbery?"

"Nothing very much," answered Dick, before either of his brothers could speak. "A girl saw a man leaving the building the evening of the robbery, but who he was, she did not know."

"And you say the box was put in the safe my uncle used to own?" went on the young man. "Of course it was locked?"

"Yes."

"Was it—er—er—was it—er—that is, did you have the same combination on it that the lock used to have?" stammered the other.

"No. I had the combination changed."

"And you haven't got the least idea then who took the bonds?" questioned Barton Pelter.

"Not so far."

"It's strange. Say, that's a fierce loss! I couldn't lose that much;" and the young man laughed nervously.

"Are you working in New York?" asked Tom, following an awkward pause.

"I haven't anything to do just now, but I am hoping to get a situation soon," answered Barton Pelter. "I've got to be going now," he added, and after a few words more, he made his way to the elevated station at the entrance to the Brooklyn Bridge.

"Evidently a pretty decent sort of a fellow," was Dick's comment, as the three brothers walked over to look at the newspaper bulletin boards. "It's too bad he has Jesse Pelter for an uncle."

"That news about our robbery seemed to astonish him," said Sam. "Did you hear him ask about the combination on the safe? He must have been wondering whether we suspected his uncle or Japson."

"That isn't strange," was Tom's comment, "when one knows what kind of rascals those two men are."

With the shadow of the loss hanging over them the Rover boys were in no mood to amuse themselves. Had it been otherwise, they might have gone to the theater or some concert, or possibly to some moving picture show. But, as it was, they spent most of their time at the offices and the hotel, and in looking around for clews.

"I received two nice letters to-day," said Dora that evening, when her husband and the others appeared, and she held up the missives. "One is from mamma, and she sends her best love to all of you. The other is from your Aunt Martha."

"And what does she say about dad?" asked Dick, quickly.

"She says there is no change in his general condition, but that he continues to worry about business matters. He wants to make sure that everything here, in New York City, is going along all right."

"Poor, old dad!" murmured Tom, and his voice was full of sympathy. "We certainly can't let him know the truth."

"Oh, not for the world, Tom!" cried Dora.

"But what are we going to do if the bonds are not found?" questioned Dick. "He has got to know it some time."

"Well, put it off as long as you can," returned his wife.

"Oh, if we could only find those bonds!" exclaimed Sam. "We've just got to do it! We've got to!"

CHAPTER XXI.
DAYS OF ANXIOUS WAITING

Another week passed without bringing anything new to light concerning the missing bonds. During that time the Rover boys received two visits from the headquarters' detectives, and were again subjected to innumerable questions.

"We're on a new tack," said one of the sleuths. "I think we'll be able to report something to you in a few days."

"You can't do it too quickly," returned Dick.

"Oh, I know that," answered the detective, with a short laugh; and then he and his companion backed themselves out.

"Say, Dick, I don't take much stock in those fellows," was Tom's comment. "They are good at talking, but it looks to me as if they didn't know where they were at."

"Exactly the way I look at it!" broke in Sam.

During that time the boys also received visits from several private detectives, all anxious to take hold of the case, but none of them willing to do so without first receiving a generous retainer.

"I am not going to pay out anything in advance," Dick told one of these fellows—a shabby looking chap. "You locate the bonds, and you'll be well paid for it."

"I don't work unless I'm paid for it," snapped the detective, and left the offices quite indignant.

"I suppose we could get a thousand detectives on this case if we were willing to put up the money," said Tom.

"It might pay to hire some first-class man," ventured Sam, "but not that sort."

"I'll call up Mr. Powell and see what he thinks of it," answered Dick. And a little later he was in communication with Songbird's uncle over the telephone.

"It wouldn't do any harm to put some first-class man on the case," said the lawyer. "If you wish me to do so, I'll put you in touch with the best detective agency in the city."

As a result of this talk, the Rovers obtained the address of a detective whose name is well-known in every large city of the United States. This man called on them the following day, and went over the case very carefully with the youths. He examined the safe and the combination lock, and then had a long talk with Kitty Donovan and her father and her mother, and also a talk with the old man who kept the little fruit stand downstairs.

"I'll do all I can, Mr. Rover," he said, when he re-entered the offices, "but you mustn't expect too much. This is certainly a mystery."

"Mr. Bronson is the most intelligent detective I've seen yet," said Sam, after the man had departed. "He handles the case as if it was a strict business proposition."

"That's what I like to see," declared Tom. "The other kind of detective is good enough for a dime or a half-dime story book, but he never makes any success of it in real life."

It must not be supposed that now they were in New York, Tom and Sam had forgotten the Laning girls. They had written to Nellie and Grace, forwarding the letters to Cedarville because Hope Seminary was on the point of closing for the season.

"Letters for both of you!" cried Dora, when they and Dick appeared at the hotel one evening after a rather strenuous day in the offices, where all had been busy forming their plans for further investments.

"Good for you, Dora!" answered Tom, and held out his hand eagerly.

"Now wouldn't you like to have it?" she answered mischievously, holding a letter just out of his reach.

"Where is mine?" demanded Sam.

"Oh, I thought you wouldn't want that so I tore it up," she answered, with a twinkle in her eyes.

"If you don't give me that letter, Dora, something is going to happen to you," went on Tom; and now he caught her by the wrist. "You know the forfeit—a kiss!"

"All right, take your letter, Mr. Can't-Wait," she returned, and handed him the missive.

"But you said you had one for me!" broke in Sam. "Come now, Dora, don't be mean."

"Oh, Sam, it's only a bill."

"A bill! You are fooling!" And then as his face fell, she did not have the heart to tease him longer, and brought the letter forth from her handbag.

As the lads had anticipated, the communications were from Grace and Nellie. In them the girls said that the session at the seminary was over, and that the day previous they had returned to their home on the outskirts of Cedarville. Both had passed in their examinations, for which they were exceedingly thankful.

"But they haven't found that four-hundred-dollar diamond ring yet," said Sam, after he had finished his letter. "It certainly is a shame!"

"It's as great a mystery as the disappearance of our bonds," was Dick's comment.

"What has Nellie to say about it, Tom?" questioned Dora, anxiously; for even though she was married and away from them, her two cousins were as dear to her as ever.

"She doesn't say very much," answered Tom. "No one has seen or heard anything about the ring."

"But what of Miss Harrow? How has she treated Nellie since the fire?"

"She says Miss Harrow has not been very well, and consequently did not take part in the final examinations. Now the teacher has gone to Asbury Park, on the New Jersey coast, to spend the summer."

"Perhaps that mystery never will be solved," said Sam. "It's a jolly shame, that's all I've got to say about it!"

After dinner that evening, as it was exceedingly warm, none of the young folks felt like staying in the hotel. Dick proposed that they take a stroll up Broadway.

"We can walk till we get tired," he said, "and then if you feel like it, we can jump into a taxi and take a ride around Central Park before we retire."

"That will be nice," returned Dora; and Tom and Sam said it would suit them, too.

As usual, upper Broadway—commonly called The Great White Way—was ablaze with electric lights. As the young folks strolled along, the great, flaring advertising signs perched on the tops of many of the buildings interested them greatly.

"I heard yesterday that some of those signs cost ten thousand dollars and more," observed Sam. "What a lot of money to put into them!"

"So it is, Sam. But think of all the money some firms spend in newspaper and magazine advertising," answered Dick.

"Some day we'll have to do some advertising ourselves," put in Tom. "That is, after we get our business in first-class running order."

"And get our bonds back," added Dick.

"Oh, say, let's forget those bonds for just one night!" entreated Sam. "I haven't been able to get a good night's sleep since I came here because of them."

The portion of Broadway where they were walking, is lined with innumerable theaters and moving picture places. They had passed on less than three blocks further, when Sam suddenly caught Tom by the arm.

"Here we are, Tom!" he exclaimed, somewhat excitedly. "Here's that moving picture."

"So it is!" returned Tom, and immediately became as interested as his younger brother. They had come to a halt before a gorgeous moving picture establishment, and on one of the billboards they saw exhibited a flashy lithograph, depicting two men struggling in a rowboat with a third man on the shore aiming a gun at one of the others. Over the picture were the words: "His Last Chance. A Thrilling Rural Drama in Two Reels."

"What is it, Tom?" questioned Dora.

"Why, that's the moving picture play we told you about—the one that we got into at the Oak Run railroad station," explained the youth. "That picture you see there was taken along the river bank back of our farm. Another picture shows the railroad station at Oak Run, with old Ricks in it, and still another ought to show the railroad train with Sam and me on the back platform. Let us go in and see it."

"Why, yes, I want to see that by all means!" declared Dick's wife. "Won't it be funny to see you boys in a moving picture!"

"Well, I don't know about this," returned Dick, hesitatingly; and he looked rather quickly at Tom. "Are you quite sure, Tom, that you want to go into a moving picture show?" he went on. He had not forgotten how Tom had once gone to a moving picture exhibition, and been completely carried away by a scene of gold digging in faraway Alaska, nor how his poor brother had for a time lost his mind and wandered off to the faraway territory, as related in detail in "The Rover Boys in Alaska."

"Oh, don't you fear for me, Dick!" cried Tom, hastily. "My head is just as good as it ever was and able to stand a hundred moving picture shows. Come on in, I'll get the tickets;" and without waiting for an answer, Tom stepped up to the little ticket booth and secured the necessary pasteboards.

CHAPTER XXII.
THE MOVING PICTURE AGAIN

The moving picture theater was fairly well filled, but the four managed to obtain seats close to the middle of the auditorium. They had entered while a slap-dash comedy was being depicted— something that set the audience laughing heartily. Then followed a parlor drama, which was more notable for its exhibition of fashions than it was for plot or acting.

"This sort of thing makes me tired!" was Tom's comment. "I like to see outdoor life much better."

Another one-reel comedy of life on the canal followed the parlor drama, and then there was flashed on the screen the words: "His Last Chance."

"Here we are!" murmured Sam, and sat bolt upright with renewed interest, while Tom did likewise. The first scene of the drama showed the interior of a farmhouse sitting-room and kitchen, and the boys easily recognized several of the men they had seen at the river and the railroad station. There followed quite a plot and a number of other scenes around the farm, and also at a stone quarry which all of the lads recognized as being located at Dexter's Corners. Then came a pretty love scene at the farmhouse, followed by a quarrel between some of the men in an apple orchard.

"Say, that's Blinks' apple orchard, just as sure as fate!" exclaimed Dick, in a low voice.

"So it is!" answered Sam. "Many's the time we've got apples there!"

The quarrel in the apple orchard was followed by a fishing scene on the river not far from Humpback Falls, where Sam once upon a time had had such a strenuous adventure. Then of a sudden came the quarrel in the boat followed by the shooting.

"Say, that looks just as it did when we saw it taken!" exclaimed Sam, enthusiastically. "This moving picture business is a great thing, isn't it?"

"It isn't just as we saw it," chuckled Tom. "They didn't show how that fellow who went overboard came up again and swam ashore."

"Oh, that would spoil the plot of the play," answered his younger brother.

Other scenes in the drama were shown, one in a barnyard full of cows being especially realistic. Then came the scene inside the railroad station at Oak Run, and all of the boys and Dora laughed heartily when they saw the look of astonishment on old Ricks' face as he peered through his ticket window at the actor who had come in for a ticket.

"I'd give a dollar to have old Ricks here looking at himself," whispered Tom. "Wouldn't he be surprised?"

"Oh, look! look!" exclaimed Dora, in a low tone. "Sam and Tom, I do declare!"

The scene had shifted suddenly, as do all scenes in moving pictures. Now was shown the platform of the Oak Run railroad station. The train was coming in, and there were Sam and Tom as natural as life, dresssuit cases in hand, ready to get aboard. The train stopped and some passengers alighted, and Tom and Sam climbed the steps of the last car.

"And look! Tom is waving his hand to some one," went on Dick's wife. "Isn't it great!"

As the train began to move away, one of the leading actors in the drama was seen to rush across the platform and grasp the rail of the last car. As he was holding himself up, another of the persons in the drama rushed after the train, shaking his fist wildly; then the train, with Tom and Sam and the moving picture actor on the back platform, disappeared from view, and in a twinkling the scene shifted back to the farmhouse once more.

"Well, we're movies' actors sure enough!" was Tom's comment, after they had seen the last of the little drama and were out on Broadway once more. "What do you think of us, Dora?"

"Oh, it was fine, Tom!" she answered. "I'd like to see it again."

"Well, they advertise it for to-morrow, too," said her husband, "so you can go in the afternoon when we are at the offices."

"I'll certainly do it!"

"I shouldn't mind seeing this picture again myself," said Sam. "If they have it to-morrow night, let's come up, Tom."

"All right, I'm willing. I suppose they are showing the thing all over the country."

The next day proved a very busy one for the three Rover boys, and for the time being the moving picture was completely forgotten. About ten o'clock, Mr. Powell came to see them regarding an investment which Anderson Rover had made during the time that Pelter, Japson & Company were his brokers. This investment now called for a further outlay of a little over seven thousand dollars, and the boys had to find some means of raising that amount.

"Now you see if we had those bonds handy, it would be an easy matter to put some of them up as collateral with some of the banks; but, as it is, it is going to squeeze us," said Dick.

"And you have got to take care of that other matter of twelve thousand dollars the middle of next month; don't forget that," broke in the lawyer. And then he added: "Of course, if you want money to help you out——"

"Thank you very much, Mr. Powell, but I think I can manage it," returned Dick.

He and his brothers had talked their plans over carefully, and had reached the conclusion that they would not ask for outside assistance unless it became absolutely necessary. They wanted to show both their family and their friends that they could "stand on their own bottom," as Dick expressed it.

"You have no word in regard to the bonds?" questioned Mr. Powell, when he was ready to leave.

"Not a word. We hired that detective you recommended, but he said it was a difficult case to handle, and that we must not expect too much."

When the Rover boys returned late that afternoon to the Outlook Hotel, they found that Dora had gone out and had not yet returned.

She had left a note on her table stating that she was going to look again at the moving picture in which Sam and Tom had taken part.

"Oh, yes, we mustn't forget to go there to-night, Sam!" cried Tom. "It's better than looking at yourself in the looking-glass, isn't it?" and he grinned.

Six o'clock came, and then half-past, and still Dora did not show herself. As the time went by, Dick began to get a little worried.

"That show ought to be out by this time," he said to his brothers. "Generally those moving picture places kind of run down between six and seven o'clock. If they are continuous they throw in some old stuff or a lot of advertising matter just to fill in the time."

"Well, maybe she stopped on the way to do some shopping," suggested Sam. "The stores must prove a great attraction to her."

"She told me yesterday that she was rather tired of shopping," answered the young husband. "You see, she went at it pretty strong at the start, so there isn't so very much left in the way of novelty. I think I'll go down and look for her;" and a minute later Dick left the apartment.

"It doesn't take much to worry him when it concerns Dora," remarked Tom, dryly.

"Well, it wouldn't take much to worry you if it concerned Nellie," retorted his younger brother.

"That's true, Sam; and the same would hold good with you if it were Grace." And then Tom dodged as Sam picked up a sofa pillow and threw, it at him.

The little French clock belonging to Dora was just chiming out the hour of seven when the two boys heard Dick and his wife coming through the hallway. They were talking earnestly, and evidently the young wife was quite excited.

"Oh, such an experience as I've had!" cried Dora, as she came in and sank down into an easy chair.

"Well now, try to calm yourself," said Dick, soothingly. "It's all over now."

"What was it about?" demanded Tom. "Did somebody hold you up, or try to steal your purse?"

"Maybe an auto tried to run over you," suggested Sam.

"No, it was none of those things," answered the young wife. "I've just had the strangest experience!"

"She met that gardener you spoke about—the fellow who lost his job at the seminary," explained Dick. "That chap named Andy Royce."

"Why, where did you meet him?" exclaimed Sam. "Did he know you?"

"Yes, he knew me quite well. When I was at Hope he used to do errands for me now and then and I tipped him quite liberally, so he remembered me," answered Dora.

"But I met him in the strangest way. He was at the subway station arguing with the ticket man, who insisted upon it that Royce had not put a ticket in the box. He wanted the gardener to put another ticket in, and Royce said he wouldn't do it. They had a very warm dispute, and a policeman came up to see what it was all about. Then, thinking that perhaps Royce didn't have any more money with him—he looked terribly shabby—I told him I would get another ticket. Then he suddenly broke down and I thought he was going to cry. I paid for another ticket, then the train came along and we both got on board."

CHAPTER XXIII.
ON THE EAST SIDE

"If Royce began to cry there must have been something radically wrong with him," declared Tom. "Dora, do you think he had been drinking? Sometimes when men drink they break down and cry, you know."

"I don't know anything about that, Tom; but I do know that he acted the strangest. I asked him if he was working, and he said no—that he had been unable to get a job of any kind. Then I questioned him about why he had left Hope, and he said it was because he could not get along with some of the hired help and with Miss Harrow."

"Say!" cried Sam. "Did he say anything about that four-hundred-dollar diamond ring that was missing?"

"Why, no, Sam. I didn't mention it, and he didn't say anything about it either. Perhaps he didn't know it was missing."

"Oh, he must know about it," broke in Tom. "It was talked about all over the place."

"Well, what happened next?" questioned Dick.

"I talked to him for awhile, and I found out that he was out of work and also out of money. I felt sorry for him, and I offered to lend him ten dollars," answered Dora. "I hope you don't think I did wrong," she went on, anxiously.

"You meant well, Dora, I'm sure of that," was Dick's quick reply, "but whether the money will do this fellow Royce any good or not, is a question. If he is a drinking man, he'll drink it up very quickly and that will be the end of it."

"Did he tell you where he was staying?" asked Tom.

"Why, yes, he gave me a slip of paper with his name and address written on it," answered Dora. "You see, I asked him to do that because I felt so sorry for him, and I thought that possibly you might be able to get him something to do;" and she handed the slip of paper over to her husband.

"'The Golden Oak House,'" read Dick from the slip. "I suppose it is one of those cheap lodging houses on the East Side," he added. "I'll keep this, although I don't see how we can help Royce. And besides that I am not certain that he deserves help. If he had remained strictly sober he might have kept his job at the seminary. But I'll think it over," he added, hastily, as he saw that Dora was much distressed.

"Did you see the moving picture again?" questioned Tom, as all prepared to go downstairs for dinner.

"Oh, yes!" and the young wife brightened a little. "It certainly is splendid, Tom! All of you ought to go and see it before they take it away."

"All right, we'll do it!" said Tom. "That is, Sam and I will go. How about it, Dick?"

"Oh, I don't know," hesitated the older brother, with a look at Dora.

"You just go, Dick," she cried, quickly. "I am going to stay here and write some letters. You go with Tom and Sam and enjoy yourself;" and so it was arranged.

The boys found the moving picture theater pretty well crowded, and they had to take seats almost in the rear. Tom and Sam were once more enjoying the spectacle of looking at themselves when they suddenly heard a young man behind them utter an exclamation.

"Hello, I know those two fellows!"

They looked around and saw sitting there Barton Pelter. He was gazing at the play on the screen with great interest.

"Come to see us in the movies, did you?" questioned Tom, as he leaned back and touched Barton Pelter on the arm. "What do you think of it?"

"Oh, so you are here!" was the reply. "Say, I didn't know you were movies' actors."

"We are not. We got into that picture quite accidentally," explained Tom. And then, as the scenes of the drama progressed, he and his brothers turned their attention to what was going on.

At the end of the photo drama there was a short intermission, during which a number of persons went out and an even larger number came in. There was a seat vacated beside the Rovers, and Barton Pelter took this.

"How are you fellows making out at your offices?" asked the young man.

"Oh, we are doing as well as can be expected," answered Dick. "You know this sort of thing is rather new to us."

"How about those missing bonds; have you located them yet?"

"No."

"That's too bad," and the young man's face showed his concern. "Have you any idea where they went to?"

"Not the slightest in the world, Pelter. It is a complete mystery," answered Tom.

"The loss of such an amount must hurt you a whole lot," ventured Barton Pelter, after a slight pause. "It would ruin some folks."

"It does hurt us a whole lot," broke in Sam. "Unless we get those bonds back—or at least a part of them—we are going to have pretty hard sledding to pull through."

"It's a shame! I wish I could do something to help you, for what you did for me," returned Barton Pelter; and his voice had a rather wistful ring in it. Then the theater was darkened and the next photo drama began.

"Are you doing anything as yet?" questioned Tom, when, at the end of this play, he saw Jesse Pelter's nephew prepare to leave.

"I've got something of an offer to go on the road as a traveling salesman for the Consolidated Cream Cracker Company," was the answer. "It won't pay very much, but it will be better than nothing;" and then the young man left.

Several days went by and the Rover boys put in all their time at business. There was a great deal to do in the way of protecting a number of rather uncertain investments which Pelter, Japson & Company had made for Mr. Anderson Rover while they were his brokers.

"It's a mighty good thing that we got after Pelter, Japson & Company when we did," was Erick's comment. "If we hadn't, they would have put us in the worst kind of a hole, even if they had remained honest. They had no more conception of what constitutes a good business risk than has a baby."

"I do hope, Dick, that we make a success of this," returned Tom.

"Oh, don't say we're going to make a fizzle of, it!" cried Sam. "We've just got to win out, that is all there is to it!"

"Right you are!"

On the following Monday afternoon there was but little for Tom and Sam to do at the offices, and the former suggested to his younger brother that they walk over to the East Side and visit The Golden Oak House.

"I've always wanted to see how things look over in that part of New York," declared Tom, "and if we run into that Andy Royce I'm going to question him and see if he knows anything about that diamond ring."

"How would he know anything about that, Tom? He wasn't near the house when the ring was lost. And besides, if he had taken the ring, he wouldn't be so poverty-stricken. He could pawn a four-hundred-dollar ring for quite some money."

"I didn't say that he might have taken the ring, Sam. But he was around the place, and he might have heard something said that would give us a clew."

"Oh, that might be possible. Anyway, we can question him, just as you said."

The walk to the East Side was quite a revelation to the Rover boys. Never had they seen such a congestion of humanity. The stores, the houses and the sidewalks seemed to be overflowing with people, while the streets were a jumble of wagons, trucks and push-carts. Every conceivable sort of a thing seemed to be on sale, and they were solicited to buy at almost every step.

"They seem to be mostly foreigners over here," was Sam's comment. "I don't know as I would care to come through here alone at night, Tom."

"Oh, you'd be as safe here as on Broadway," was the reply. "These people are poor, but you'll find them just as honest as anybody."

The boys had with them the card that Andy Royce had given to Dora, and it did not take them long to find The Golden Oak House. It was an old-fashioned, frame building located on the corner of a narrow and exceedingly dirty alleyway. Downstairs there were a saloon and a pawnshop. The so-styled office and the sleeping apartments were on the three floors above.

"Not a very inviting place," were Sam's words, as he looked the resort over. "Tom, do you think we had better go in?"

"Oh, I don't think it will hurt us," was the answer. "Come ahead!"

Ascending the narrow and exceedingly dirty stairs, the boys passed through a dingy hall to where a glass door was marked "Office." Inside they found a small counter and rail, behind which a man in shirt-sleeves sat smoking a cigar and reading a sporting paper.

"Is there a man stopping here named Andy Royce?" asked Tom, as the man dropped his paper to look up at the newcomers.

"I think there is, but I don't believe he's in now," was the answer. "Want to leave any word for him?"

Tom thought for a moment. "Yes," he answered. "I will leave a message." And taking out one of his cards, he wrote on it: "I'll call here Tuesday afternoon at about five o'clock to see you."

"Hope you've got work for that fellow. He needs a job the worst way," said the hotel man, as he took the card.

"I don't know about a job for him, but perhaps I can help him," answered Tom. And then he and Sam left the place.

They had just reached the sidewalk when they beheld Andy Royce coming towards them. The former gardener of Hope Seminary was partly under the influence of liquor, and several children were annoying him by pulling at his coat and calling him names.

"You go 'way an' leave me alone," mumbled the man. And then, as he caught sight of the Rovers, he tried to brace up.

"Hello, you here!" he exclaimed.

"Yes, we want to talk to you, Royce," answered Tom. Then he motioned the children away, and led the former gardener of the seminary towards the alleyway beside the hotel.

CHAPTER XXIV.
ANDY ROYCE'S CONFESSION

"Want to talk to me, eh?" mumbled Andy Royce. "What you want, anyhow?"

"See here, Royce! what is the use of your drinking like this?" broke in Sam. "Is that the way to use the money my brother's wife loaned you?"

"I ain't been drinkin'," mumbled the man. "That is, I ain't had much."

"You've had more than is good for you," put in Tom. "A man like you ought to leave liquor alone entirely."

"Maybe I would—if I had a job," growled the former gardener. "But when a man ain't got no work an' no friends it's pretty hard on him;" and he showed signs of bursting into tears.

"See here, Royce, you brace up and be a man!" cried Tom. "Because you haven't any position is no reason at all why you should drink. You ought to save every cent of your money and make it last as long as possible."

"All right, just as you say, Mr. Rover," mumbled the man.

It was evident to the youths that the man was in no condition to think clearly. Evidently he had been drinking more or less for a long while, for his face showed the signs of this dissipation. His clothing was ragged, and he was much in need of a shave and a bath. Certainly he did not look at all like the gardener he had been when he had first come to Hope.

"See here, Royce, I want to ask you a few questions," said Tom. "Do you remember about that diamond ring that disappeared at Hope while you were there?"

"Eh? What?" stammered the former gardener. "Who said I knew anything about that ring?" and he showed confusion.

"Did you hear anything about it at all?" asked Sam.

"Say, is this a trap?" mumbled the man. "If it is, you ain't goin' to ketch me in it. Not much you ain't!"

"Look here! If you know anything about this, Royce, you tell us," declared Tom, struck by the man's manner.

"I ain't goin' to say nothin'! I didn't steal the ring!" cried Andy Royce.

"But you know something about it, don't you!" declared Tom, sharply; and caught the former gardener by the arm.

"Say, you lemme go! I ain't goin' to tell you a thing!" cried the man, in alarm. "You ain't goin' to trap me like this. I know wot I'm doin'. Lemme go, I say!" and he tried to break away.

"You're not going a step, Royce, until you tell us the truth," declared Tom, now quite satisfied in his own mind that the former gardener was holding something back.

"If you took that ring you had better confess," broke in Sam.

"I didn't take it, I tell you," muttered Andy Royce. "You ain't goin' to get nothin' out o' me! This is a put-up job! I won't stand for it!" And once again he tried to break away. But each of the boys held him fast.

"I guess the best we can do is to call a policeman and have him locked up," declared Tom, with a knowing look at his brother. He had no intention of having the former gardener arrested, but thought the threat would frighten the fellow. And this was just what it did. At the mention of being locked up, Andy Royce's courage seemed to leave him.

"No! No! Don't you do it! Please, gents, don't have me locked up!" he whined. "I didn't take the ring!"

"But you know what became of it," declared Tom, sternly. "So if you didn't take it, who did?"

"No—nobuddy took it," stammered Andy Royce.

"But it's gone," came quickly from Sam.

"Well, if you've got to know the truth, I'll tell you," growled the man, staring unsteadily at the boys. "It's in Miss Harrow's inkwell."

"Miss Harrow's inkwell!" repeated Tom, incredulously.

"Did you put it there?" questioned Sam.

"I did."

"Well, why in the world did you do that?" asked Tom, and made no effort to conceal his wonder.

"Why did I do it?" mumbled the man, unsteadily. "I did it to git Miss Harrow into trouble. I knowed she was responsible for the ring."

"Then you were in the office," declared Sam.

"Sure, I was there! If I wasn't, how would I a-seen that ring? I was told that Miss Harrow wanted to see me, an' I went to the office just at the same time when she came down to the stables where me and two of the other men had had a quarrel. It wasn't my fault, that quarrel wasn't, but them other fellers put it off on me and said 'twas because I had been drinkin'," continued Andy Royce, with a whine. "When I got to the office there wasn't nobuddy around. I saw that diamond ring layin' on the desk, and I picked it up— —"

"You were going to steal it?" broke in Tom.

"No, I wasn't, Mr. Rover. I may drink a little now an' then, but I ain't no thief," went on Andy Royce. "I never stole anything in my life. I knowed that ring, because I saw Miss Parsons wear it more than once. I was mad at Miss Harrow for the way she treated me, an' just out of mischief I took the ring an' opened the inkwell an' dropped it in. It was in the inkwell that had red ink in it, an' the ring went plumb out o' sight."

"And you left the ring in the inkwell?" queried Tom.

"Sure I did! Then, not to be seen in the office, I slipped out in a hurry, an' left the seminary by the back door an' ran to the stables. Miss Harrow was there. She had told me that she was goin' to discharge me if there was any more trouble, so I knowed wot was comin'. Then I quit, an' come away," concluded Andy Royce.

"Well, of all the things I ever heard of, this takes the cake!" was Sam's comment.

"If this fellow's story is true, the ring ought to be in the inkwell yet," said Tom. "That is, unless the well was washed out and put away for the summer. In that case the person who cleaned the well ought to have found the ring."

"Sounds almost like a fairy tale," went on Sam. "I don't know whether to believe it or, not."

"It's the truth!" cried Andy Royce.

"We'll believe it when we see the ring," returned Tom, grimly. "I guess the best thing you can do, Royce, is to come with us."

"Please don't have me arrested! I've told you the truth, sure!"

"If you'll come with us and behave yourself, we won't have you arrested," answered Tom. "But we are not going to let you get away until we have found out if your story is true."

"We might telegraph to the seminary at once," suggested Sam. "Do you know who is in charge there during the summer?"

"Why, I heard Nellie say that Miss Parsons took charge—the teacher who left the ring with Miss Harrow."

"Then why not telegraph to her?"

"We'll do it! But this fellow has got to come with us until we are sure his story is true."

Andy Royce demurred, but the boys would not listen to him. They accompanied him to his room upstairs, and made him pack up his belongings and pay his bill. Then, somewhat sobered by what was taking place, the gardener accompanied them downstairs and to the street. Here the boys hailed a passing taxicab that was empty, and ordered the driver to take them as quickly as possible to the Outlook Hotel.

"It certainly is a queer story," said Dick, who had just arrived from the office, "but it may be true. People do queer things sometimes, especially when they are under the influence of liquor. He probably had a grudge against Miss Harrow, and thought the disappearance of the ring would get her into trouble, just as he said."

"Oh, I hope they do find the ring!" cried Tom. "It will be great news for Nellie."

It was arranged that Andy Royce should accompany Dick and Sam to the smoking room of the hotel, and remain there until Tom had telegraphed to Hope Seminary and received a reply.

"You had better run upstairs and see Dora first," suggested Dick, "and make sure as to who is in charge at the seminary. If there are two persons there, you had better telegraph to both of them so that they can unite in looking for the ring."

Dora was in a flutter of excitement when told of what had occurred. She remembered about Miss Parsons, and said that there was also a housekeeper named Mrs. Lacy in charge. Armed with this information Tom sent off two telegrams, each reading as follows:

"Look for missing diamond ring in Miss Harrow's red-ink inkwell. If found, answer at once.

Thomas Rover,
"Outlook Hotel,
"New York City."

"They were mighty funny telegrams to send," said Tom, when he rejoined his brothers in the hotel smoking room. "Perhaps they won't know what to make of them."

"I am afraid we'll have to wait quite a while for an answer," returned Dick.

"Oh, I don't know. They can telephone the messages up to the seminary from the telegraph office."

"They'll find the ring just as I said unless somebuddy cleaned out the inkwell and took it," declared Andy Royce, who was rapidly sobering up because of the turn of affairs.

As it was getting late, it was decided that Dick should go to dinner with Dora as usual, while Tom and Sam took the former gardener to a corner of the restaurant for something to eat.

"I don't feel much like filling up," said Sam. "I'm on pins and needles about an answer to those messages you sent, Tom."

"Exactly the way I feel, Sam. But we'll have to have patience, I suppose."

The meal at an end, Dora went upstairs, and Dick rejoined his brothers and Andy Royce in the smoking room. Tom had left word at the hotel telegraph office that any message which might come in for hire must be delivered at once.

"Here comes a bellboy now!" cried Dick, presently.

"Mr. Rover! Mr. Rover!" cried the boy, walking from one group of persons to another.

"Here you are! here you are, boy!" cried Tom, leaping up; and in another moment he had a telegram in his hand and was tearing it open to see what it contained.

CHAPTER XXV.
MORE TELEGRAMS

"Who is it from, Tom?"

"Read it out loud!"

Such were the exclamations from Sam and Dick as their brother scanned the telegram in haste.

"Hurrah! they've found it!" broke out Tom. "This is the best yet!"

"Good!"

"Fine!"

"This is from Miss Clara Parsons," went on Tom, "the teacher who owned the ring. Here, you can read the telegram if you want to," and he passed the sheet over. The message ran as follows:

"Ring found in inkwell. Perfect condition. Did Miss Laning put it there?

"Clara Parsons."

"Short and sweet, but it tells the story," was Dick's comment. "Say, I'm mighty glad of this," he added, and his face showed his pleasure. "That clears Nellie, Tom. You'll have to let her know at once."

"I sure will!" exclaimed the brother. "But say, did you notice what Miss Parsons wants to know—if Nellie put the ring in the inkwell? Talk about nerve!"

"You can't exactly blame her, Tom, because she knew nothing of Royce's visit to the office; and as you sent the message, and you and Nellie are so intimate."

"Oh, I understand, Dick; and I shan't blame her. I'm too happy to blame anybody," and Tom's face broke into a broad smile. "I'm going to send a telegram to Cedarville this minute."

"Didn't I tell you gents the ring was there?" broke in Andy Royce. "I told you the truth, didn't I?"

"You did, Royce," answered Dick.

"A'n' wot about it, are you goin' to lemme go?" questioned the former gardener, eagerly.

"Not just yet," broke in Tom.

"Why not? You can't hold me for stealin' when there wasn't nuthin' taken."

"That is true, Royce, but we want you to sign a confession as to just how that ring got in the inkwell. If you don't do that, the seminary authorities may still think it was placed there by Miss Laning."

"Oh, I don't want to put nuthin' off on Miss Laning's shoulders," answered the former gardener. "If you want a confession from me so as you can clear her, go ahead!"

"Wait here until I've sent that telegram," Tom said, hastily; and rushed off once more to the telegraph office, where he sent the following to Nellie:

"Ring recovered. Was hidden in inkwell by Royce.
We have gardener's confession. Hurrah! Will write
particulars.

"Tom."

"I hope she gets that before she goes to bed to-night," mused the youth. "If she does it will make her sleep so much better."

There was a stenographer's office attached to the Outlook Hotel, and late as it was, the young lady was found at her typewriter, pounding out a letter for a commercial traveler. As soon as this was finished, the stenographer was asked to take down whatever Andy Royce might have to tell. The former gardener was brought in, and repeated the confession he had previously made. This was typewritten as speedily as possible, and then Andy Royce signed the confession in the presence of one of the hotel clerks and a notary who lived at the hotel.

"Now I think that fixes it," said Tom. "Miss Parsons won't be able to go behind that confession."

"Are you goin' to let me go now?" asked the former gardener of Hope.

"Yes, you can go, Royce," answered Tom. "But wait a minute. How much money have you left of that ten dollars my brother's wife let you have?"

For reply the man dove down in his pocket, and brought out some change.

"Eighty-five cents."

"That's all?"

"Yes."

"See here, if I stake you with another ten dollars, will you give me your word not to drink it up?"

"I will, Mr. Rover, I will!" exclaimed Andy Royce, earnestly.

"All right, then, here's the money;" and Tom brought out two five-dollar bills and placed them in the man's hands. "Now look here, unless you can find something to do, you come here and see me again in a few days."

"But see here, Tom," interposed Dick, in a low voice, "I don't think we can use Royce in anyway. Why not let him go? As a gardener he is out of place in a big city like New York."

"I want him to stay here for two reasons," answered Tom. "In the first place I want him on hand in case the authorities at the seminary need him. In the second place, I am going to put the matter squarely up to Miss Harrow. She thought Nellie guilty, and she may have thought Royce worse than he really was. Perhaps I can get her to give Royce another chance. I think he would be all right if he would only let drink alone."

"The same old warm-hearted Tom as of old!" responded Dick. "All right, have your own way about it."

After the former gardener had departed the boys went upstairs to join Dora, and then Tom and Sam sat down to write letters of explanation to Nellie and Grace; and these epistles were posted before the youths retired for the night.

"Oh, how glad Nellie must be to have this weight off her shoulders!" exclaimed Dora. "It must have been awful to be suspected of taking a ring."

"I guess Miss Harrow will be relieved, too," answered Tom. "I wonder where she is stopping in Asbury Park."

"I think I know," returned Dick's wife. "She and some of the other teachers usually go to the Claravale House."

"I'll take a chance and telegraph to her," went on Tom. "It won't cost much and it may relieve her mind. Those folks up at the seminary may wait to send a letter." And going downstairs once more, Tom wrote out another brief telegram, and asked that it be sent off immediately.

"If only we could clear up this mystery of the missing bonds as easily as we did this ring business!" came from Sam, when he and Tom had said good-night to Dick and his wife.

"I'm afraid that's not going to be so easy, Sam. Sometimes I think that we'll never hear a word more about those bonds;" and Tom heaved a deep sigh.

"Oh, but, Tom, if we don't get those bonds back we'll be in a hole!" cried the youngest Rover, in dismay.

"We may not be in a hole exactly, Sam; but we'll have a tough job of it pulling through," was the grim response.

Tom had worried more about the missing ring than he had been willing to admit to his brothers, and now that this was off his mind, he, on the following morning, pitched into business with renewed vigor. He and Dick had their hands full, going over a great mass of figures and calculations, and in deciding the important question of how to take care of certain investments. Sam did what he could to help them, although, as he frankly admitted, he did not take to bookkeeping or anything that smacked of high finances.

"I was not cut out for it, and that is all there is to it," he declared. "But I am willing to help you all I can."

Sam had gone off on an errand, leaving his brothers deep in their figures, when the office boy announced a visitor.

"Mr. Mallin Aronson," said Dick, glancing at the visitor's card. "Oh, yes, I've heard of him before. He and father had some stock dealings a year or so ago. Bring him in."

Mr. Aronson proved to be a small, dark-complexioned man, with heavy eyebrows and a heavily-bearded face. He bowed profoundly as he entered.

"Mr. Richard Rover, I believe?" he said, extending his hand.

"Yes, Mr. Aronson. And this is my brother Tom," returned Dick.

"Very glad to know you;" and the visitor bowed again. "I presume you know what brought me here," he went on, with a bland smile.

"I can't say that I do," returned Dick.

"Your father—is he not here?"

"No, he is at home sick."

"Is that so? I am very sorry to hear it. Then you are transacting his business for him?"

"Yes, my brother and I are running this business now."

"And yet you said you did not know why I had called," continued Mr. Aronson, in apparent astonishment. "That is strange. Did not your father tell you about his investment in the Sharon Valley Land Company?"

"I never heard of the company before," returned Dick, promptly.

"I heard my father mention it," put in Tom, "but I never knew that he had made any investment in it."

"What? How surprising!" ejaculated the visitor. "He has something like fifteen thousand dollars invested in that concern, for which I have the honor to be the agent. He has another payment to make on the investment, and that payment falls due just a week from to-day. Some time ago he asked me if that payment might not be deferred. I put it up to the managers of the company, and they have now sent me word that the payment will have to be made on the day that it falls due."

"And how much is that payment?" faltered Dick.

"Twenty thousand dollars."

CHAPTER XXVI.
IN WHICH THE GIRLS ARRIVE

Both of the Rover boys stared blankly at the visitor. His announcement had come very much like a clap of thunder out of a clear sky. For the moment neither of them knew what to say.

"I am sorry you did not know about this," pursued Mallin Aronson, when he saw by their looks how much they were disturbed. "Perhaps your dear father was taken sick so quickly that he did not have a chance to explain the situation."

"He hasn't been well for a long while, but I thought he had turned over all his business affairs to us," answered Dick. "It is queer that we have no record of this Sharon Valley Land Company investment," he added, turning to Tom.

"Have you gone over all the papers, Dick?" questioned the brother, quickly.

"The most of them. That is, all that I thought were of any importance. There are a great number that I haven't had time to look at yet. You know how numerous father's investments are."

"If you have no record of the transaction here, can you not ask your father about it?" questioned Mr. Aronson, smoothly.

"He is too sick to be disturbed, Mr. Aronson," answered Dick.

"Well, if you care to do so, you can stop at my office and look over the account there," went on the visitor.

"And you say this twenty thousand dollars has got to be paid a week from to-day?" asked Tom.

"Yes, Mr. Rover. The management will grant no extension of time."

"Supposing it isn't paid?" questioned Dick.

At this suggestion Mallin Aronson shrugged his shoulders and put up his hands.

"I am sorry, but you know how some of these land company people are," he returned. "This money must be paid in order to clear the land. If it is not cleared the company has the right to sell your father's interest to others. As I said before, he has paid fifteen thousand dollars. What his interest would bring if sold to somebody else, I do not know."

"Probably not very much," returned Dick, quickly. "Probably some of the land company people would buy it in for a song," he added, bitterly.

"Well, Mr. Rover, that is not my affair," and Mr. Aronson shrugged his shoulders. "I came in only to serve you notice that the twenty thousand dollars will have to be paid one week from to-day."

"Where are your offices, Mr. Aronson?"

"You will find my address on the card," was the answer. "If you wish any more information, I shall be pleased to give it to you;" and then the visitor bowed himself out.

It was a great blow, and the two youths felt it keenly. Ever since the loss of the sixty-four thousand dollars in bonds they had been struggling with might and main to cover one obligation after another. To do this had taxed about every resource that Dick could think of aside from borrowing from friends without putting up any security— something the youth shrank from doing.

"Say, Dick, this is fierce!" exclaimed Tom. "What are we going to do about it?"

"I don't know yet," was the slow reply. "I can't understand why father didn't mention this investment to me."

"He must have felt so sick that he forgot all about it. You don't imagine that there is anything wrong about it?"

"Oh, no! I guess it is all straight enough. Aronson must know that he couldn't get any such money out of us unless everything was as straight as a string."

"Perhaps Mr. Powell could get the twenty thousand dollars for us."

"Maybe he could. But that isn't the point, Tom. I told you before that we want to 'stand on our own bottom.' Besides, it isn't a fair thing to ask any one to put up money like that without offering good security."

"But we don't want to lose the fifteen thousand dollars that father has already invested."

"I know that, too. It's a miserable affair all around, isn't it?" And Dick sighed deeply.

When Sam came back from his errand he brought news that under ordinary circumstances would have interested his brothers very much.

"I was coming through Union Square Park when whom should I see on one of the benches but Josiah Crabtree!" he exclaimed.

"Crabtree!" cried Tom. "Then he must be out of the hospital at last! How did he look?"

"He looked very pale and thin, and he had a pair of crutches with him," answered Sam. "I didn't see him walk, but I suppose he must limp pretty badly, or he wouldn't have had the crutches."

"Did you speak to him?" questioned Dick.

"No. At first I thought I would do so, but he looked so down-and-out that I didn't have the heart to say anything and perhaps make him feel worse."

"Do you suppose he has any money?" asked Tom.

"He didn't look as if he had. But you never can tell with such fellows as Crabtree—he was a good deal of a miser."

"What a misspent life his has been!" was Dick's comment. "I am mighty glad that he didn't get the chance to marry Mrs. Stanhope."

"Right you are, Dick!" returned Tom. "He'd make a hard kind of a father-in-law to swallow!"

It did not take long for Dick and Tom to acquaint Sam with the new money problem that confronted them, and the youngest Rover became equally worried over the situation.

"I think we had better write to Uncle Randolph and see if he can find out a little about this land company affair from father without, of course, worrying him too much," suggested Dick. "There may be some loophole out of this trouble—although I am afraid there isn't."

"All right, we'll do it," said Tom, and the letter was written at once, and sent to Dexter's Corners with a special delivery stamp attached.

On the following afternoon when Tom and Sam got back to the hotel, a surprise awaited them. Going up to the suite occupied by

Dick and Dora, the brothers found themselves confronted by Nellie and Grace.

"Oh, Tom!" was all Nellie could say. And then coming straight forward she threw herself into his arms and burst into tears.

"Now—now, don't go on this way, Nellie," he stammered, not knowing what to say. "It's all right. They've got the ring and you are cleared. What's the use of crying about it now?"

"Oh, but—but I can't help it!" sobbed the girl. "You don't know how I have suffered! I couldn't sleep nights, or anything! Oh, Tom! it was grand—the way you got that gardener to confess;" and she clung to him tighter than ever.

"And to think he put the ring in the inkwell!" cried Grace. "What a ridiculous thing to do!"

"He must have done it on the spur of the moment," said Sam. "But say, I'm mighty glad that affair is cleared up!" he added, his face beaming.

Then all of the young folks sat down, and the story had to be told once more in all of its details.

"I just had to come on! I couldn't stay home after I got the telegram and the letter," explained Nellie, "so I sent a telegram to Dora."

"We planned to surprise you," put in Grace.

"And it is a surprise, and a nice one," returned Sam. Soon Dick, who had been somewhat detained, came in, and then there was more excitement.

"Well, what about accommodations for the girls?" asked Dick, who never forgot the practical side of matters.

"Oh, that is all arranged, Dick," answered his wife. "I have a room for them, and as your wife I am to be their chaperon;" and she smiled brightly as she passed her hand over his forehead. "Poor boy, with so much to do!" she added, affectionately.

It was a happy gathering, and for the time being the Rover boys did their best to forget their troubles. They had a somewhat elaborate dinner, and then Tom and Sam took the newcomers out for a walk up "The Great White Way." Dick said he would remain at the hotel with his wife, as he wanted to write some letters.

"Might as well let them have their fling," he said, after the others had departed. "That's the way we wanted it before we were married;" and he gave his wife a hug and a kiss.

Of course the girls from Cedarville had a great deal to tell, and Tom and Sam had a great deal to relate in return. The two couples strolled on and on, and it was near eleven o'clock before they returned to the Outlook Hotel.

"And so you are going to be a real business man, are you, Tom?" said Nellie, during the course of the walk.

"I am going to try to be, Nellie," he answered. "Of course it is something of a job for a fellow who is full of fun to settle down. I need help." And he looked at her wistfully.

"Oh, Tom, if you would only settle your mind — —"

"There's no use in talking, Nellie, I won't be able to settle down in the really-and-truly fashion until I am married," retorted the fun-loving Rover. "You have got to be the one to settle me."

"Tom Rover, if you talk like that I'll box your ears!"

"All right, anything you say goes, Nellie. Only tell me, aren't we going to be married some time this Fall or Winter?"

"Tom!"

"Well, aren't we?"

"Oh, maybe. But you come on! We are out for a walk, and here we are standing stock-still in the middle of the sidewalk with folks all around us. Come on! If you don't come I will leave you;" and Nellie started on, dragging Tom with her.

CHAPTER XXVII.
THE MYSTERY OF THE SAFE

Dick was at his desk sorting out his morning mail. He was rather downcast, for the past two days had brought no news regarding the missing bonds. On the other hand, he had received word from his uncle that the investment in the Sharon Valley Land Company was a perfectly legitimate one, and that Mr. Aronson's claim would have to be met.

"And how we are going to meet it, I don't know," said Dick, in speaking of the matter to his brothers. "It certainly is tough luck to have these obligations pouring in on us at just this time."

"Well, there is one bright spot in uncle's letter," returned Sam. "He says dad is feeling somewhat better. I am mighty glad of that."

"I guess we all are," broke in Tom. "Just the same, I agree with Dick. The financial outlook is mighty gloomy."

There were other letters besides business communications for the boys. Songbird had written, and so had Spud; and Dick had likewise a long epistle from Bart Conners, who in years gone by had been the young major of the Putnam Hall cadets. But just now Dick had no heart to read these communications. He felt that he must give his entire attention to the business in hand. One letter in a plain envelope was in a handwriting entirely unfamiliar to him. He cut open the envelope hastily to see what it might contain. A glance at the single sheet inside, and his face showed his interest.

"Look at this, boys!" he cried; and then read the following:

"'Look over your safe very carefully. You may discover something to your advantage.'"

There was no signature.

"Who sent that?" came from Sam and Tom simultaneously.

"I don't know. It isn't signed."

"'Look over your safe very carefully. You may discover something to your advantage,'" repeated Tom. "Say! that looks as if somebody knew something about the robbery!" he went on, excitedly.

"We have looked over the safe a dozen times," returned Sam. "It hasn't furnished the slightest clew."

"We'll go over it again," broke in Dick, who had already left his desk and gone to the strong-box. He worked at the combination for a few moments, and pulled open the safe door.

"Maybe we ought to have a light here," suggested Tom. "It is rather dark in this corner."

"Wait, I can fix that," said Sam, and reaching for a droplight that hung over the desk, the youngest Rover commenced to unfasten the wire by which it was held in position. By this means he was able to shift the light so that it hung directly over the opening of the strong-box.

"Nothing unusual about the door or the combination that I can see," said Tom, after all had made a careful inspection.

"And the sides seem to be all right," added Sam. "Maybe it's the back or the bottom."

"If it wasn't so heavy we might be able to swing the safe around away from the wall," said Dick. "But wait, hold that light closer, Tom, and I'll see if I can find out anything from the inside."

Dick was now on his knees and feeling around the back of the safe with his hand. Presently he found a crack, and inserting his fingers he gave a push. Much to his astonishment a portion of the safe back slid upward.

"Hello, I've found something!" he ejaculated. "There is a hole in the back of this safe!"

"You don't say so!" cried Sam; and he and Tom peered into the steel box.

Then Dick continued to work around with his hand, and presently was able to slide another section of the safe back upward. He now found that he could touch a piece of board which evidently took the place of some plaster that had formed part of the office wall.

"There must be a small trap door there, leading to some place outside," said the oldest Rover boy. "We'll go into the hall and have a look."

It did not take the eager youths long to reach the hallway of the building, and once there, all three hurried to the spot where they thought the opening might be located. Soon they came to the little closet which the janitor had once mentioned to them—a small place in which was located a sink, and also a number of brooms, brushes, and cleaning cloths.

The closet was dark, but Dick had brought along a box of matches, and a light was quickly made. A corner containing some brooms and cloths was cleaned out, and the boys soon located a piece of board about eight inches square, covered with a sheet of tin painted the same color as the wall.

"It's as plain as daylight!" cried Tom. "The thief didn't have to open the safe door at all. He simply came in here, removed that board, slid up the back section of the safe, and took out what he wanted."

"And the fellow who did it——" broke in Sam.

"Was either Pelter or Japson," finished Dick.

"Then you think this letter came from——" Tom started to say.

"That young fellow whose life you saved—Barton Pelter," answered Dick.

"By the rudder to Noah's Ark, I think you are right!" burst out Tom. "Why, it's as plain as the nose on your face! Don't you remember how worried Barton Pelter looked when we told him the bonds were missing, and how he asked us at the moving picture show if we had gotten them back yet? More than likely he knew how this safe was fixed—he used to come here, you know, to see his uncle——"

"I believe you're right, Tom," came from Sam, "because if he didn't do it, who did?"

"I think I can make sure of this," returned Tom. "Let us go back to the offices."

Tom had taken possession of one of the desks in the place, and in one of the pigeonholes he had placed a number of letters, including the one received while at college from Jesse Pelter's nephew. This he now brought forth, and compared the handwriting with that of the letter just received.

"It's the same hand," he affirmed. And after an examination the brothers agreed with him.

"If Barton Pelter wrote that letter we ought to locate him without delay," was Sam's comment. "He may know just where the missing bonds are."

"Or else where we can locate his uncle and Japson."

"Wait a minute!" cried Dick. "You forget that Japson has been away from New York for some time. The detective told me that, and said it was positive. So that would seem to put the thing off on Pelter's shoulders; and I think Pelter is just the man to do such a thing. You'll remember how bitter he was against us when we exposed him."

"Then let us locate Jesse Pelter without delay," broke in Tom. "It ought to be easy, unless he is in hiding."

"If he's got our bonds he'll certainly do his best to keep out of our way," returned Dick, grimly. "I think the best we can do first of all is to locate Barton Pelter and make him tell us all he knows."

"He said he had a chance of a position as a traveling salesman."

"Did he say for whom?"

"He mentioned 'The Consolidated Cream Cracker Company,' whatever that is."

"Let us call them up and find out," said Dick.

By consulting the telephone directory, the boys were soon in communication with the cracker company in question. They were informed that Barton Pelter had been taken on as a salesman the day before, and had left that evening for a trip through the Middle West. It was not known on what train he had departed.

"Nothing doing here," said Tom. "They don't even seem to know what town he is going to stop at first."

"I think we had better call up Mr. Bronson, and tell him about this and put him on the trail of the Pelters," answered Dick.

The detective was as astonished as the boys had been when he saw the hole in the back of the safe.

"This is certainly one on me," he confessed, frankly. "I looked that safe over very carefully, too. I should have discovered that;" and his face showed his chagrin.

Then he was told about the Pelters and about Japson, and he agreed with the Rovers that he had best try to locate Barton Pelter and his uncle without delay.

"I'll put a man on the trail of the young fellow who went West," he said, "and as soon as he sends me any word regarding Jesse Pelter I'll go after that fellow, and I'll also let you know what I'm doing;" and so it was arranged.

CHAPTER XXVIII.
JOSIAH CRABTREE ONCE MORE

When the boys arrived at the hotel that evening the girls had much to tell them. Nellie had received a letter from Miss Harrow, in which the teacher had frankly begged her pardon for having suspected the girl of taking the diamond ring.

"It is a lovely letter," said Nellie. "I never thought that she could humble herself in that fashion."

"I've got an idea; in fact, I've had it for some time," came from Tom. "I had Royce in this afternoon to see me. He is very anxious to get work. I've half a notion to ask you to write to Miss Harrow and see if they won't take the fellow back at the seminary."

"I am willing to write such a letter, Tom," answered the girl. "And if they won't take Royce back, perhaps I can get my father to give him work at our farm; although I know he is more of a gardener than he is a farmer."

But the most important news the two girls and Dick's wife had to tell was that on a shopping tour after lunch they had walked into Josiah Crabtree.

"We came face to face with him in front of a show window," explained Dick's wife. "I was so startled for the minute that I did not know what to say. Oh, Dick! he was on crutches, and he did look so pale and thin I couldn't help but feel sorry for him!"

"He has evidently suffered a great deal," put in Grace. "In fact, he said as much. He seemed to be utterly downcast. He didn't look like the dictatorial teacher he used to be at all."

"What did he have to say?" questioned Sam.

"Oh, he was quite confused at first, but he did ask about Dora's mother—if she was well—and then he said he understood that you three were going into business together. He said he hoped you would be successful."

"The idea of old Crabtree saying that!" burst out Tom. "It's enough to make a fellow think the end of the world is coming."

"Did he say what he was doing, or what he proposes to do?" questioned Dick.

"He said he had received a tentative offer of a position in a boys' school in Maine," answered Nellie, "but he did not know whether he was going to take it or not. My idea is that he is too poor to even go to Maine. And he had on such an old, rusty, black suit!"

"Say! Did he say where he was stopping?" questioned Dick, eagerly, struck by a sudden idea.

"No, he did not."

"Too bad! I'd like to see him as soon as possible."

"Why, what's up now, Dick?" questioned Sam.

"I want to ask him if he knows anything about Jesse Pelter—where the fellow has gone to."

"It isn't likely. I don't think those two parted the best of friends."

"Most likely not. Still Crabtree may know where Pelter keeps himself."

"I'll tell you what you might do, Dick," suggested Tom. "You might send Crabtree a couple of letters, one addressed to the General Delivery here, and another simply addressed to New York City; then you'll run two chances of striking him."

"I'll do that," answered the older brother; and sent off the communications without delay. In each of them he asked Josiah Crabtree to call at his offices as soon as possible.

"Do you think you can make him open up if he comes?" questioned Sam.

"I think so—that is if I make it worth his while. If Crabtree is down on his luck he will most likely be willing to do anything for money."

Two days went by, and the boys waited anxiously for some word from the detective in regard to the whereabouts of the Pelters. But no word came in, and they were as downcast as ever. In the meanwhile Dick, aided by the others, stirred around as best he could in an endeavor to take care of their finances.

"I've got the small things all taken care of," Dick said to Tom and Sam, on the evening of the second day. "But what I am going to do about that twenty thousand dollars we must pay the Sharon Valley Land Company, and that other claim Mr. Powell spoke about, I don't know. It looks to me as if we were going to get into a hole, unless I'm able to get some of our friends to help us out."

The one bright spot on the horizon was the news received from home, which was to the effect that their father's health was improving. He had gone downstairs and walked around the garden, and also taken a short ride in the automobile. Moreover, his mind seemed to be much brighter than it had been for a long while past.

On the following morning, when the three youths were at the offices discussing the situation, Bob Marsh came in.

"A man to see you," announced the office boy. "A man on crutches named Crabtree."

"Show him in!" exclaimed Dick. And then he added hastily to his brothers in a lower tone: "Now let me engineer this, please. I think I know how to handle him."

"Go ahead, Dick," responded Tom; and Sam nodded.

Josiah Crabtree hobbled in on his crutches, with his hat in his hand. Evidently he was weak and nervous. His thin face had lost much of its former shrewdness and cunning, and he looked quite downcast.

"Good morning, young gentlemen," he said, in a somewhat cracked voice. "You sent me a letter. I just got it at the post-office."

"Sit down, Mr. Crabtree," returned Dick, and offered the former teacher of Putnam Hall a chair.

"Thank you." Josiah Crabtree sank down on the seat, resting his crutches against his knee. "You have the same offices that Pelter, Japson & Company had, I perceive," he continued, allowing his eyes to rove around.

"Yes, Mr. Crabtree," answered Dick. "By the way, do you know where Mr. Pelter is just now?"

"You said you wanted to see me about some particular business," said the former teacher. "Perhaps we had better get at that first."

"Well, I might as well admit, Mr. Crabtree, that what I wanted to see you about is this. I want to know if you can tell me where Mr. Jesse Pelter is just now."

"Oh, is that all!" And Josiah Crabtree's face showed his disappointment.

"That is all at present."

"Humph! Supposing I don't care to tell you where he is?"

"Now see here!" pursued Dick, earnestly. "If I understand matters aright, Mr. Crabtree, Jesse Pelter is no longer a friend of yours. When you went to the hospital he practically deserted you, isn't that right?"

"If is!" exclaimed the former teacher, bitterly. "He left me in the lurch, and not only that, he didn't give me the money that was rightfully coming to me."

"Exactly so! Now then, why shouldn't you help us to locate him?"

"Well—er—well—er—supposing I did help you?" returned Josiah Crabtree, hesitatingly.

"If you will do that, Mr. Crabtree, I'll make it well worth your while," responded Dick, quickly. "I may as well admit to you that we wish to get hold of Mr. Pelter as soon as possible. We want him to clear up a certain transaction. If you can put me into communication with him to-day, I'll give you fifty dollars."

At the mention of fifty dollars Josiah Crabtree's eyes lit up. Evidently he had not seen that amount of money for some time.

"You'll give me fifty dollars?" he repeated.

"I will."

"There is no fooling about this, Rover?"

"Mr. Crabtree, did I ever deceive you?" And Dick looked the former teacher squarely in the eyes.

"I don't think you did, Rover. So you want to find Jesse Pelter, and you'll give me fifty dollars if I'll help you do it? All right, I'll take you up. I don't think Pelter is aware that I know where he is, but I do;" and Josiah Crabtree smiled grimly.

"Where is he?"

"He told Japson that he was going down East, most likely to Boston. But he didn't do any such thing; he hung around New York for awhile and then he went to Philadelphia, and he's down there now, I am thinking, unless he took a boat for Europe."

"What? Was he going from Philadelphia to Europe?" broke in Tom.

"So I understood. Although why he didn't go from New York is a mystery—the service is so much better."

"Have you any idea where he is stopping in Philadelphia?" questioned Dick.

"He usually stopped with a distant relative of his—a man named Crowley Pelter."

"Then that's all I want to know for the present, Mr. Crabtree," announced Dick. "If we can locate him I'll let you know and then the fifty dollars will be yours."

"How soon are you going to look for the man?" asked the former teacher, curiously.

"At once," was Dick's quick reply. "Leave me your address, and as soon as we hear anything I'll let you know." And a few minutes later the boys brought the interview to an end.

CHAPTER XXIX.
THE JAPANNED BOX

"Now to find out where Crowley Pelter lives!" said Dick.

The train carrying the three Rover boys from New York to Philadelphia was rolling into the big, smoky station. It was about two o'clock in the afternoon, and the youths had dined on the train while making the journey. They had left the offices in charge of Bob Marsh, stating that they would most likely be away for the rest of the day. At first Dick and Tom had thought to leave Sam behind, but the latter had insisted on going along. It had been a two hours' run to the Quaker City.

"Let's look at a telephone directory," suggested Tom.

"Oh, you don't want to telephone to him, do you?" queried Sam. "That might put Jesse Pelter on his guard."

"We won't telephone, we'll simply look for the address," answered his brother.

But there proved to be no Crowley Pelter in the telephone directory, so the boys had to consult a regular directory. They found that the man lived quite a distance out, in the Germantown section.

"Let's hire a taxi, and get out there as fast as we can," suggested Dick. Now that they were actually on the trail of the missing broker he was anxious to bring the pursuit to an end.

Outside the railroad station taxicabs were numerous, and the boys quickly hired one of the best of the machines and gave the driver directions where to go.

"And don't lose any time," ordered Dick.

"I'll run as fast as I dare," returned the chauffeur.

The ride to Crowley Pelter's residence took a good three-quarters of an hour. The place was a small but well-kept one on a corner.

"I guess I had better go in alone," suggested Dick. "If I need you I'll whistle or wave my handkerchief;" and then he ran up the front steps and rang the bell. A tall, angular woman, wearing large spectacles, soon answered his summons.

"Good afternoon," said Dick, politely. "Is this Mr. Crowley Pelter's residence?"

"Yes, sir."

"I believe Mr. Jesse Pelter is staying here. Can I see him?" went on Dick.

"Mr. Jesse Pelter was staying here, but he has just gone—he went about an hour ago."

"Is that so!" cried Dick. "Can you tell me where he went to?"

"Well, I—er—I don't know," faltered the woman, and eyed Dick sharply.

"I have a very important message for him," Dick hastened to say. "I must see him at once."

"Oh, in that case you'll find him down at the docks. He has engaged passage on the *Princess Lenida* bound for Liverpool."

"And when does the *Princess Lenida* sail?" asked Dick, quickly.

"I don't know exactly. Either this afternoon or to-morrow morning."

"And you are sure he has gone to the steamer?"

"Oh, yes. He sent his baggage off this morning, and he said he would not be back."

"Thank you, Madam." And without another word Dick turned and left the residence.

As he did this he saw a man he knew hurrying along the street. The man stopped when he caught sight of Dick and the two boys in the taxicab.

"Why, you here, Mr. Bronson?" cried Dick.

"Hello! how in the world did you fellows get here!" exclaimed the detective the Rovers had hired but a short time before. "Are you on the trail of Pelter, too?"

"We are," answered Dick. "How did you learn he had been here?"

"Had been! Do you mean to say he has left?"

"Yes. The woman who came to the door told me he had left about an hour ago. He is going to sail on the *Princess Lenida* for Liverpool either this afternoon or to-morrow morning."

"Say, then we want to get after him at once!" cried the detective.

"I agree on that," answered Dick. He turned to the chauffeur. "Do you know the dock from which the *Princess Lenida* sails?" he questioned.

"Sure I do! I've been there many a time," answered the taxicab driver.

"Then take us there just as quickly as you can," said Dick. "Never mind the speed laws. If you are held up we will pay the fine."

"We won't be held up—not if I show this," said the detective, and exhibited the badge pinned to his vest. Then Dick and Mr. Bronson jumped into the taxicab, and away the turnout went at top speed back to the heart of the city.

"How did you get here?" questioned Tom, of the detective while riding along.

"As I said I would, I got into communication with one of our men out West, and he went after that Barton Pelter. He got him in Dayton, and made him confess that he had sent that note to you. Then he told our man that his uncle was most likely here in Philadelphia; so I came on at once to see if I could locate the man."

"If only we can catch him before he sails!" cried Sam.

"Oh, we've got to do it!" put in Tom.

Soon the taxicab reached the crowded thoroughfares of Philadelphia. They made several turns, crossing the track of the street cars, and finally came to a halt near the river front.

"There's the dock you want," said the chauffeur, pointing with his hand.

"Is that the *Princess Lenida?*" questioned Dick, quickly, indicating the upper works of a steamer, which could be seen over the dock buildings.

"I think so, sir."

"Come on, then!" cried Tom. "Sam, you pay the fellow, will you?"

"All right!" was the quick reply. And then Tom and Dick hurried after Mr. Bronson, who was already entering the dock building.

Had they been alone the Rovers might have had some difficulty in gaining entrance to the dock; but the detective led the way, showing his badge; and soon the party found themselves at the gang-plank of the steamer. Here Sam rejoined them.

From the purser they learned that Jesse Pelter had engaged stateroom Number 148.

"But I can't say if he is aboard or not," said the steamer official. "You see, we are not to sail until nine o'clock to-morrow morning. There was some talk of sailing this afternoon, but we have been delayed. Do you want me to send to the stateroom for you?"

"Oh, no, we'll go there ourselves," returned the detective, quickly. "I don't want to alarm him if I can help it."

"I guess you are after him," said the purser, grimly.

"We certainly are!" answered Tom.

It was an easy matter to locate stateroom Number 148, which was on the main deck forward. The entrance was in a narrow passageway, and close at hand was a door opening on a narrow walkway between the staterooms and the ship's rail.

"Wait a moment," whispered the detective, and stepped outside. He was now close to a shuttered window of the stateroom engaged by Jesse Pelter.

From the room came a murmur of voices, and without speaking further the detective motioned for the Rover boys to join him beside the window. Although the slatted shutter was up, evidently the glass of the window had been let down its full length, for those outside could hear what was said within with ease.

"That proposition is all right as far as it goes," they heard, in Jesse Pelter's voice. "But I can't see, Haywood, where you ought to have fifty per cent. of the returns."

"I do!" answered somebody else—evidently the man called Haywood. "I'm running all the risk, it seems to me."

"Not so very much of a risk," went on Jesse Pelter. "Sixty thousand dollars' worth of those bonds are unregistered."

"All very true. But for all you know the numbers may be advertised as stolen. If so, I may get pinched when I offer them."

"Not if you are careful and work the thing in the right kind of a way," pursued the former broker.

"Well, I'll tell you what I'll do," returned Haywood. "I'll take a third and not a dollar less. Now let us go over the bonds and check them up," he continued. And then followed a rustling of numerous papers.

"Don't you think we have heard enough?" whispered Dick, to the detective.

"All that is necessary, Mr. Rover," was the answer. "Stand close by me," the detective continued, "and be prepared to rush them the instant the door is opened."

Having thus spoken, Mr. Bronson stepped back through the passageway, and knocked sharply on the stateroom door.

"Who's there?" came in nervous tones from Jesse Pelter.

"A telegram for Mr. Pelter!" cried the detective, in a high-pitched, boyish voice.

"Oh!" came from within; and then the key was turned in the lock, and the door was opened several inches.

The next instant the detective threw his weight against the barrier, and forced it back. He leaped into the stateroom, and the three Rover boys followed him.

"Hi, what does this mean?" cried Jesse Pelter, as he was forced backward against a washstand.

"It means that your game is up, Pelter!" cried Tom.

"We've caught you just as we wanted to!" added Dick.

"And you're not going to get away either," came from Sam, as he managed to close the stateroom door and put his back against it.

Mr. Bronson had said nothing. He held the former broker with one hand, and produced a pair of handcuffs with the other. Then came a double click, and Jesse Pelter found himself handcuffed.

"See here, you let me out of this!" stormed the man named Haywood. "I haven't done anything wrong. You let me go!" And he started for the door.

"Not much! You stay where you are!" cried Tom, and gave the fellow a shove which sent him sprawling backward over a berth.

In the meanwhile Dick's quick eyes had located the japanned box partly filled with the missing bonds. Other bonds lay on the berth and on the floor. The oldest Rover boy lost no time in gathering up the precious documents, and placed them in the box.

"I tell you I want you to let me go!" spluttered Haywood. "I haven't done anything wrong!"

"See here, Grimes," broke in the detective, sternly, "you sit right where you are. I know you, and you ought to know me;" and the detective took a step forward and looked the man full in the face.

"Oliver Bronson!" murmured the man who had agreed to dispose of the stolen bonds. "How did you get onto this game?"

"You'll find out about that later, Grimes."

"Is his name Grimes?" questioned Tom.

"That's one of his names. He is also known as Haywood, and likewise Slippery Peter. He used to work in Pittsburgh and Washington; but I heard some time ago that he was trying his games on in Philadelphia."

"See here, Rover, can't we—er—fix this little matter up somehow?" faltered Jesse Pelter.

"We can, and we will—in court," answered Dick, coldly.

"Oh, but see here——"

"Don't waste your breath, Pelter. We let you go on those other charges, but we are not going to let you go on this one," interrupted Dick. "This was a downright steal, and you have got to take the consequences. Mr. Bronson, what do you want to do with them?"

"One of you had better call in a policeman," returned the detective. "Then we'll take them to headquarters. I think this is quite a catch," he continued. "The authorities have been trying to fasten something on Grimes for a long while."

"Humph! You haven't fastened this on me yet," growled the sharper mentioned.

"Don't worry. You'll get what's coming to you," returned the detective.

Sam slipped out, and in a few minutes returned with a policeman. Then a call was sent in for a patrol wagon, and in this the entire party was taken to the police station. A formal charge was entered against the two criminals, and they were led away to separate cells. Then came several formalities before Dick and his brothers were allowed to take possession of the japanned box with its precious contents. The bonds were gone over with care, and it was ascertained that not one was missing.

"Oh, this is great!" cried Tom, his face beaming. "I feel like dancing a jig."

"So do I," returned Sam. "Dick, don't you think we had better send word to New York?"

"Oh, we'll take the next train back, Sam, and surprise the girls," answered the oldest brother.

"I'll remain behind in Philadelphia, and take charge of this case," said Mr. Bronson. "Now that you have your bonds back, I suppose you'll want to fix up some of those financial matters that you mentioned."

"We certainly do," answered Dick.

And after a few words more, the boys bade the detective good-bye, and hurried to take a train back to the metropolis.

CHAPTER XXX.
MRS. TOM ROVER—CONCLUSION

"And you got back all the bonds, Dick? How, splendid!"

It was Dora who uttered the words, shortly after the arrival at the Outlook Hotel of the three Rovers. Dick had had the japanned box under his arm, and now held it up in triumph.

"Yes, we've got them all back, and those that don't go to the bank as collateral security for a loan are going to a safe deposit box," answered Dick. "I won't take any more chances with an office safe."

"Especially not that office safe," put in Sam, pointedly.

"And what are you going to do with Jesse Pelter?" questioned Nellie.

"We are going to put him where he belongs—in prison," answered Tom. And it may be as well to state here that in due course of time Jesse Pelter and his partner in crime, Grimes, *alias* Haywood, were tried and sentenced to long terms in prison. At this trial it was brought to light that Barton Pelter had known about the hole in the back of the safe, but had had absolutely nothing to do with the taking of the bonds. Jesse Pelter was very bitter against his nephew for exposing him, but the Rovers told the young man that he had done exactly right, and he said that he thought so, too. As soon as the trial was over Barton Pelter returned to the Middle West, where he did fairly well as a traveling salesman for the cracker company.

The next few days following the recovery of the bonds proved busy ones for the Rovers. Some of the bonds were put up at a bank as collateral security for a substantial loan, and with this money Dick took care of the Sharon Valley Land Company investment, and also the investment brought to his attention by Mr. Powell.

"Now we are on the straight road once more!" declared Dick, after these matters and a number of others had been cleared up.

"And I'm mighty glad of it," returned Tom, with a beaming face. "I think we all ought to go off and celebrate. What's the matter with a trip to Coney Island, or something like that?"

"Wow! I thought he was going to suggest a honeymoon trip for himself and Nellie," cried Sam, mischievously.

"Say, young man, don't get so previous!" retorted Tom, growing red in the face. "Just the same, that's coming a little later," he added, quickly.

"Provided Nellie is willing," went on the youngest Rover, teasingly.

"Oh, don't you worry about that, Sam. By the looks of things you'll be in the same boat some day."

"Well, a fellow might do worse," answered Sam, coolly.

The days to follow were full of combined business and pleasure for the boys. When they were not at the office they were with the girls, and all took numerous trips to various places of amusement in and out of the metropolis. As was to be expected, Tom was the life of the party, and the way he "cut up" was "simply awful," as Nellie declared.

"Well, I can't help it," was the way the fun-loving Rover explained his actions. "I've got to let off steam or 'bust,'" and then he did a few steps of a jig, finishing by catching Nellie up in his arms and whirling her around in the air.

Of course the boys had lost no time in sending word to the folks at Valley Brook Farm that all business complications had been straightened out, and that everything at the offices was running smoothly. In return came back word that Mr. Anderson Rover was feeling stronger than ever, and hoped ere long to be well enough to visit the city.

> "But I don't expect to do much in business," wrote Mr.
> Rover. "I am going to leave that entirely to Dick and
> Tom. I understand that Tom expects before a great
> while to get married, and when that happens I want to
> form The Rover Company, and take him and Dick in
> with me, Sam, of course, to come in later, after he has
> finished at college, although he won't have to take an

active part unless he wishes to do so. My best love to
all of you, and may you have no more trouble."

"Dear old dad!" murmured Tom, when he had perused this communication, and for a moment his voice grew husky and his eyes moist.

Now that it had been definitely settled that Tom and Nellie were going to be married, Sam wanted to know if the date couldn't be set early enough so that he could be on hand before returning to Brill. This bolstered up Tom's plea for an early ceremony, and it was decided that the wedding should come off the first week in September.

Then followed great preparations on the part of Nellie and the others. Mrs. Laning and Mrs. Stanhope came down to New York, and numerous shopping tours were instituted, in which the boys had no part. Then the Lanings and Mrs. Stanhope returned to Cedarville, and Tom and Sam went back to the farm.

During those days, as busy as they were, Nellie and Tom had not forgotten Andy Royce. Letters had been exchanged between the young folks and those in authority at Hope Seminary, and at last it was arranged that the gardener should be taken back and given another chance. He promised faithfully to give up drinking.

The Rover boys had also had several visits from Josiah Crabtree. They had found out that the former teacher of Putnam Hall was practically down and out, and, although he was not deserving of their sympathy, all felt sorry for him, and so not only did they give him the fifty dollars as Dick had promised, but they also presented him with a new outfit of clothing. Then Josiah Crabtree departed, to accept the position as a teacher which had been offered to him.

"Where are you going to live after you are married, Tom?" questioned Sam. "Are you going to the Outlook Hotel, too?"

"Not much, no hotel life for me!" returned Tom. "Nellie and I talked it over with Dora and Dick, and we have taken an apartment together on Riverside Drive, a pretty spot overlooking the Hudson River. We are going to keep house together, and we'll all be 'as snug as a bug in a rug.'"

"Oh, that will be fine!"

"Some day, Sam, I suppose we'll be taking in you and Grace," went on Tom, with a grin. "Well, we'll do it even if we have to get a larger apartment."

It had been decided that the wedding should take place in the Cedarville Union Church—a little stone edifice where Dick and Dora had been married, and which for years had been the church home of the Lanings and the Stanhopes. Nellie and Tom had a host of friends, and it was a question how so many could be accommodated in such a small building.

"Well, if they can't get in, they'll have to stand outside," said Tom, when talking the matter over. "We'll do the best we can." And then the invitations to the affair were addressed and sent out.

As was to be expected, the wedding presents were both numerous and costly, rivalling those received by Dora and Dick. Mr. Anderson Rover duplicated the silver service given to his oldest son, and Dick and Sam joined in forwarding a handsomely decorated dinner set. As Uncle Randolph and Aunt Martha had given Dick a set of encyclopedias, they sent other books to Nellie, but not forgetting a specially-bound volume of the uncle's book on scientific farming. In addition to all this came a bankbook from Mr. Anderson Rover with an amount written therein that was the duplicate of the amount he had presented to Dora and Dick.

"I knew he'd do it, Nellie," said Tom, when, with their heads close together, the pair looked at the bankbook. "It's just like dad."

"It's too perfectly splendid for anything, Tom!" returned the girl, her eyes beaming. "When I get the chance I'm just going to hug him to death!"

Nellie and Grace had always been Mrs. Stanhope's favorite nieces, and now that lady sent a set of beautifully embroidered linen, some of which had been in the Stanhope family for several generations. And to this gift Mr. and Mrs. Laning added some cut glass dishes of the latest design. Then came from Captain Putnam of the school which the boys had attended so many years, a revolving bookstand, and with it a box of books, each volume from some particular youth who in the past had been a cadet at Putnam Hall—twenty-four volumes in all, each with a name in it that brought up all sorts of memories to Tom as he read it.

"One of the nicest gifts the Old Guard could have given me!" was Tom's comment. "It must have been some job to get that set of books together. Why, some of those fellows are miles and miles away! They are scattered all over the United States."

Many of the students at Hope had remembered Nellie, and even Miss Harrow sent her a small water-color picture. From the boys of Brill came half a dozen presents—some useful and some ornamental. Even Tom's former enemy, Dan Baxter, who was now his friend, had not forgotten him, and sent a pair of napkin rings, suitably engraved. Tom's own present to his bride was a magnificent diamond brooch, which pleased Nellie immensely.

And then came the great day, full of sunshine and with a gentle breeze blowing from the West. Tom and his family, including his father, who now felt almost as strong as ever, were located at the old Stanhope home with a number of their friends, while many of Nellie's relatives and friends were stopping with the Lanings at their farm. Other friends of both the young folks were located at the Cedarville Hotel.

To follow the time set by Dick and Dora, it had been decided to hold the wedding at high noon. As before, the church was decorated with palms brought up from Ithaca. Soon the guests began to assemble, until the little edifice was crowded to its capacity. Captain Putnam was there in full uniform, and with him over a score of cadets. From Brill came at least a dozen collegians led by Spud and Stanley. Even William, Philander Tubbs was on hand, in a full-dress suit of the latest pattern, and with a big chrysanthemum in his buttonhole. There were several bridesmaids led by Grace, while Sam was Tom's best man. The wedding party was preceded by, a little flower girl, and a little boy beside her who carried the wedding rings on a pillow.

Nellie was on her father's arm, daintily attired in white charmeuse with her tulle veil trimmed in orange blossoms, and her girl friends declared that she was the prettiest bride they had ever seen. The ceremony was a short one, and at the conclusion Tom gave his bride such a hearty smack that every one present had to smile.

"A fine wedding, don't you know!" was William Philander Tubbs' comment, when a number of the guests were on their way to the Laning home, in carriages and automobiles.

"Yes. And Tom has got a fine girl!" answered Songbird.

"Where's the poetry for the occasion, Songbird?" queried Stanley.

"Oh, I am reserving that for the wedding dinner," was the answer. And it may be mentioned here that at the proper time the would-be poet recited an original poem of half a dozen verses, written in honor of the occasion.

"Say, Dick, we've got to give Tom a send-off," whispered Sam to his big brother, after the Laning home had been reached.

"We sure will give him a send-off!" returned Dick, who had not forgotten what had taken place when he and Dora had departed on their honeymoon.

"I wish I didn't have to go back to Brill," went on the youngest Rover, rather wistfully, and with a sigh.

"Oh, your term at college will soon come to an end, Sam. You may have lots of fun." What fun Sam did have, and what further befell the boys will be related in the next volume of this series, to be entitled "The Rover Boys on a Tour; Or, Last Days at Brill College."

The wedding dinner, participated in by all the relatives and a great number of friends, was a huge success. An orchestra had been engaged for the occasion, and after the meal there was dancing by the young folks for several hours, both indoors and on the broad veranda of the homestead.

"Where are you going on your wedding tour, Tom?" asked Spud.

"We haven't decided yet," was the quick reply. "We're thinking something of going to the north pole, but we may go to the moon instead;" and at this answer there was a general laugh.

"They are going to slip away if they can," was Sam's comment to half a dozen of his chums, a little later. "We'll have to be on our guard."

All of the young folks had provided themselves with rice, confetti, old shoes, and strips of white ribbon with which to celebrate the occasion—the ribbon being for the purpose of decorating the young couple's baggage. Sam had also provided a placard which read: *"Are we happy? We are!"* and this was nailed to Tom's trunk.

"Where are they?"

This was the cry that went up in the middle of one of the dances. Tom had slipped off into a side room, and Nellie had followed. Now both of the young folks were missing.

"They are going out the back way!" cried Dick.

"Everybody watch the stairs and the doors!" exclaimed Sam. "We mustn't let them get away from us!"

There was a general scramble, commingled with shrieks of laughter as the young folks did their best to locate the missing couple. Then of a sudden came a wild toot from an automobile horn.

"There they are!"

"Come on, everybody!"

There followed a wild scramble from the house to the lane leading to the roadway. In the lane was an automobile belonging to the Cedarville garage, and run by a chauffeur. On the back seat were Tom and Nellie, waving their hands gaily.

"Good-bye, everybody! Sorry we have to leave you so soon!" yelled Tom.

"We'll be back some day! Good-bye!" added Nellie.

"After them! After them!" yelled Dick and Sam; and then all of the young folks hurried up the lane, pelting those in the automobile with rice and old shoes.

"We might go after them in another auto," suggested Spud.

"You'll never catch that machine," returned one of the Putnam Hall cadets. "That's the fastest car around Cedarville. Tom knew what he was doing when he hired it."

The automobile with the newly-married pair had already reached the highway. Those left behind waved their hands gaily, and Tom and Nellie, standing up in the tonneau, waved in return. Then with another loud toot of the horn the automobile dashed onward, and disappeared around a turn of the road.

"Well, good-bye to them, and may they be happy!" said Anderson Rover, who stood on the veranda watching the departure.

"Yes, I think they deserve to be happy," answered Mrs. Laning, who stood beside him, wiping the tears from her eyes. "Nellie is a good girl, and Tom is a good boy in spite of his liking for fun. I do hope they get along in life!"

"Come on back and finish the dance," said Sam to Grace. And then catching her arm tightly, he whispered: "It is our turn next, isn't it?"

"Maybe, Sam," she returned, in a low voice Already the band was striking up, and soon the young folks had resumed their dancing; and here for the time being we will leave them, and say good-bye.